He was looking at her intensely. His gaze zeroed in on her mouth.

Her pulse stuttered to a halt for a brief second, before resuming triple-time. Their time on the balcony seemed an age ago now, but when he looked at her like that it was as if it had been yesterday.

She took his empty beer bottle, pleased to be doing something, breaking the eye contact. She headed into the kitchen, desperate for space, and almost jumped when she realized he'd followed her.

Callum stood in the doorway, suddenly clear about why he'd come tonight. He wanted her. He had since the Ball, and he didn't want to pretend he didn't any more. 'I want to make love to you.'

Dear Reader

Welcome to the very last in my Brisbane General trilogy! Set in my home town of Brisbane, this trilogy explores the lives and loves of three nurses, the Winters sisters—Beth, Rilla and Hailey. And three very special doctors—Gabe, Luca and Callum.

I've always wanted to write a linked series, and was thrilled when my editor suggested it. I love catching up with previous characters and being familiar with a particular setting. And Brisbane General is a beauty. Being a nurse, I can tell you there's no place quite like a hospital to bring out real emotions and make people realise what is truly important in life.

In THE SINGLE DAD'S NEW-YEAR BRIDE, Hailey and Callum throw their hearts into the ring. The new Head of Paediatrics, Callum Craig, is a widower with a six-year-old son, Tom, who is recovering from leukaemia. Hailey is damaged from a relationship with another man and his child. Neither wants to complicate their already complicated lives. But sometimes fate has other things in store, and life throws curve balls. And it all begins with a kiss at the hospital's New Year's Eve Ball!

I hope you enjoy their story, and their eventual realisation that life is for living and love can't be denied.

I've loved the whole experience of creating this hospital and these wonderful characters. I wish all my readers health, happiness, and above all love.

Amy Andrews

THE SINGLE DAD'S
NEW-YEAR BRIDE

BY
AMY ANDREWS

MILLS & BOON
Pure reading pleasure™

First published in Great Britain 2008
Harlequin Mills & Boon Limited,
Eton House, 18-24 Paradise Road, Richmond, Surrey TW9 1SR

© Amy Andrews 2008

ISBN: 978 0 263 19920 8

Set in Times Roman 10½ on 12¾ pt
15-1108-48648

Printed and bound in Great Britain
by CPI Antony Rowe, Chippenham, Wiltshire

Amy Andrews has always loved writing, and still can't quite believe that she gets to do it for a living. Creating wonderful heroines and gorgeous heroes and telling their stories is an amazing way to pass the day. Sometimes they don't always act as she'd like them to—but then neither do her kids, so she's kind of used to it. Amy lives in the very beautiful Samford Valley, with her husband and aforementioned children, along with six brown chooks and two black dogs. She loves to hear from her readers. Drop her a line at www.amyandrews.com.au

Recent titles by the same author:

DR ROMANO'S CHRISTMAS BABY*
TOP-NOTCH SURGEON, PREGNANT NURSE*
THE OUTBACK DOCTOR'S SURPRISE BRIDE
FOUND: A FATHER FOR HER CHILD
THE ITALIAN COUNT'S BABY

Brisbane General Hospital

To Joyce Russell, who has read all my books.
Thanks, Joycie. Your support means so much.

CHAPTER ONE

HAILEY WINTERS had never felt so isolated in her life. Which was no mean feat considering that the ballroom held about four hundred people. Music from an eighties retro band blared out from the stage and party-goers danced amidst the strobe lighting while others milled around, conversing in small groups. Her table companion chatted away, unaware of her total distraction.

She sighed. She'd been keeping herself together so well these last few months. Moving on. But surrounded by couples while single on New Year's Eve was not her idea of fun. Her sisters, Beth and Rilla, had insisted she attend the hospital ball, insisted it was time she got out, insisted she stopped telling them she was fine and demonstrate it. So she had agreed—reluctantly—because she wanted to prove to them she *was* fine and, of course, she'd also never been able to say no to them.

And they meant well, but she just wasn't the party type. Any more. She watched Beth and her husband Gabe across the table. He was saying something to her, his mouth pressed against her ear, and her sister laughed, looking adoringly up at him. Gabe's lips moved again and Beth opened her mouth, giving him, a faux scandalised look.

Oh, please, get a room!

She turned her attention to Rilla and Luca. Her Italian brother-in-law and her middle sister with matching olive complexions looked like two peas in a pod. She saw Rilla's eyes widen as Luca's hand suspiciously disappeared from view and Hailey rolled her eyes. *Make it two rooms.* If anything, newly reconciled and expecting their first baby, they were even more lovey-dovey than Beth and Gabe.

New Year's Eve was for lovers and unfortunately she just didn't fit the bill. Not that she wanted to. Not that she was looking. She'd moved on. And being alone for the rest of her life was infinitely more appealing than having her heart stomped all over again. Yet, still, she felt…restless tonight. Out of place.

Hailey realised Ronald Archer, an acquaintance of her father's, had stopped droning on and was looking at her expectantly for a reply. She brought her wandering thoughts back into order and re-entered the conversation.

A minute later, still listening to Ronald, Hailey froze as something brushed against her stockinged leg beneath the table. She almost stopped breathing as the tiny interloper scratched its way up further under her floor-length ballgown.

Hailey shuddered. *Please, don't let it be a spider.*

'Excuse me for a moment,' she said politely to Ronald, before scraping her chair back, knocking it to the floor and leaping away from the table. She stamped her feet on the floor like a horse, trying to shake the unfortunate creature loose.

Thankfully, with the Brisbane General's annual New Year's Eve Ball in full swing, there were few witnesses to her wild jig.

'Goodness, dear, whatever is it?' Hailey's table partner enquired.

'Something just crawled up my leg, Mr Archer,' Hailey said, inspecting the floor for the insect that had dared defile her expensive French stockings. It was difficult to see anything in the muted lighting of the ballroom. 'Some kind of bug or insect.' She shuddered.

'Or maybe something even more dangerous? Like a small child, perhaps?'

Hailey looked up from the floor as she heard her companion's laughter. A boy sat on his haunches just under the table, his mouth and eyes wide open in his pale face, a small torch in one hand, a toy truck in the other. He was wearing a white shirt with a fat bow-tie and had remorse stamped on every adorable feature. He may as well have had the word 'Guilty' tattooed on his forehead.

'Oh,' Hailey said, the screaming bug-phobic girlie inside instantly retreating now the danger was apparently nonexistent. 'Hello, there.' She smiled.

The little boy smiled back at her and Hailey could almost hear his audible expiration as it slowly dawned on him from the grins on everyone's faces that he wasn't going to be in trouble. He opened his mouth to say something but didn't get the chance.

'Tom!'

Hailey saw uncertainty twist his small brow into a deep furrow as she turned to face the exasperated-looking man striding towards them. He was tall with hair so short he looked like he'd lost a battle with a lawnmower and after only two seconds' perusal Hailey could see he filled a tuxedo better than any other man there.

Better than Gabe. Better than Luca. And her brother-in-laws were bona fide hotties.

Callum Craig took one look at the scene—an upturned

chair, his son under a table, several adults looking down at him—and groaned inwardly. What had Tom been up to now? He'd only lost sight of him for a minute. How had he managed to create such havoc so quickly?

Hailey put her hand out to halt the man's progress and took a step towards Tom, offering him her outstretched hand. 'It's fine,' she assured him hastily, as the little fingers wormed into hers. Hailey's heart lurched at the, oh, so familiar action and she gave an automatic reassuring squeeze as she tugged gently and pulled his little body in close to hers.

'I'm terribly sorry,' Callum apoligised, righting the chair and noting the woman's protective stance. 'I hope he wasn't a nuisance.'

'Not at all,' Hailey dismissed quickly.

'Damn fine eye if you ask me.' Ronald Archer chuckled. 'He picked the best set of legs at the table.'

Hailey blushed as Callum looked at his son askance. 'Tom—what did you do?'

'I was just playing with my truck under the table and her shoes were so sparkly and her legs so shiny I just had to make them a road.'

Tom flicked his torch on and shone it at Hailey's shoes to demonstrate. The whole table, now caught up in the melodrama, looked down too. Hailey lifted the hem of her long gown, revealing diamanté-encrusted, strappy heels. They caught the light magnificently. The silver threads in her stockings also shimmered enticingly.

'Aren't they bootiful, Daddy?'

Hailey looked at the boy's father, amused to know that this man could be put on the back foot by a little boy. She raised an eyebrow.

Callum saw the challenge in the woman's gaze, saw the amusement sparkling there. He felt a nudge of awareness spike his bloodstream as the brief glimpse of the woman's feet and ankles dared him to explore higher. He allowed himself a few lazy seconds to thoroughly discover the delights of her slinky red dress, the close-fitting bodice, the deep V of her cleavage.

The whole package from her toes to the dusting of freckles on her upturned nose seemed pretty good from where he was standing. Very, very delectable. 'I agree, Tom,' Callum said, holding the stranger's gaze. 'Superb.'

Hailey felt heat envelop her. She swallowed, her throat suddenly as dry as the Sahara. She felt…devoured. She blinked. And blinked again before sanity returned. For crying out loud. *The man had a kid*. And no doubt a wife.

''Perb,' Tom repeated, smiling up at Hailey.

She tore her eyes away from the magnetism of the man's heat-seeking gaze. 'Thank you, young man,' Hailey curtsied. 'I got them from Paris.'

Tom's eyes rounded again. 'You know Paris Hilton?'

Hailey blinked as the little band of onlookers tittered. She caught Rilla's wink as she turned to look up at Tom's father, whose sinful-looking lips were pressed together hard trying to stay in a straight line. 'Paris Hilton?' She raised her eyebrows.

Callum shrugged. 'He has an inquisitive nature. We watch the news together.'

'Paris, France.' Hailey turned back to face Tom. 'I bought them in a gorgeous department store and they cost me a fortune.

'Well, I like them. They're 'perb.'

Hailey beamed at him, his words disarmingly innocent,

obviously proud of himself to have remembered the new word. He reminded her of another little boy at another time and her smile slipped slightly.

Happy thoughts, Hails. Happy thoughts.

'Nevertheless, Tom, people's legs aren't racetracks,' Callum chided gently. 'I'm sure you scared the lady half to death.'

Callum could see no harm had been done but even for a six-year-old, Tom was exceptionally impulsive. His illness and extended stay in hospital hadn't done much for his social skills. 'Apoligise to the lady... Er, I'm sorry...I don't know your name.'

'Hailey,' she supplied. 'Really, it isn't necessary. I'm sure he's just bored out of his brains.' What was the man doing at a ball with a child anyway? Hadn't he heard of babysitters? Where was his mother?

'Tom,' Callum prompted, ignoring Hailey's protestations.

Hailey's heart went out to Tom as she watched his little shoulders slump. He shuffled his feet, his eyes cast downwards, finding a spot on the carpet exceedingly fascinating as he flicked his torch on and off.

'I'm sorry, Hailey. I only wanted to drive my truck on a glittery road.'

Hailey crouched down until she was at eye level with Tom. She placed a finger under his chin and gently raised his face. She wanted to haul him into her arms and hug him. She removed her hand and clamped her arms firmly by her side, giving him a big grin instead.

'Hey, that's OK. It's the first time anyone's wanted to race a car along my legs. I'll cherish the memory for ever.'

Tom's eyes grew wide again. 'Really? For ever and ever and ever?'

She nodded her head solemnly. 'To infinity and beyond.'

'Wow.' Tom exhaled. 'Did you hear that, Dad?'

'Come on, Tom.' Callum squeezed his son's shoulders. From this vantage point he could see right down into Hailey's deep cleavage and he was acutely aware he hadn't admired a woman's décolletage for quite a few years. He was gawking like a horny teenager. 'We have to keep mingling.'

Now was not the time to have his libido roar to life. They were in a new city, with a new job, a new house and a new school. And Tom had only finished his grueling treatments six months ago. There was much to occupy him. He really didn't have time for sparkly shoes and racetrack legs.

Hailey looked up from her crouched position and caught the man's steady stare. She felt the heat again and almost toppled backwards from the blast. Tom and his father departed and it took Hailey a moment to collect herself before she could stand. And even then her hands trembled and her insides felt decidedly unsettled.

Hailey escaped outside to the balcony ten minutes before the big countdown began. The very last thing she wanted was to be inside when the clock reached midnight. Beth would have Gabe, Rilla would have Luca and she…she would have eighty-not-out Ronald Archer.

So, she'd wait it out here and then say her goodbyes. Her sisters would protest but neither of them could say she hadn't fulfilled her promise to attend. She knew they were only trying and that they'd been worried about her since her return from the UK. All her family had. But no amount of parties was ever going to erase what had happened. That took time and she *was* moving on. She was.

OK, maybe she hadn't exactly made much of an effort

to enjoy herself tonight as her sisters had hoped. Maybe she hadn't met her perfect match, as they'd hoped. But she was there, wasn't she? An image of Tom's father flashed before her and she banished it. Damn the man! Her gaze had followed him around the room all night.

So, the man looked good in a tux. So, he'd looked at her like he'd wanted to eat her up. She wasn't some innocent Cinderella, hanging around in her glass slippers, waiting for her prince to pull up on a white horse.

Been there, done that. Fairy-tale crushed into the dust. *Over it. So, over it.*

Or at least she'd thought she was until that man and his son had barged into her glowingly successful recovery process.

She gave herself a mental shake and wandered over to the ornamental railing. A breeze was blowing and it ruffled her hair, lifting it off her shoulders. The moon was three-quarters full and an entrancing milky glow bathed the beautifully landscaped gardens below. She inhaled deeply, a waft of heavily scented camellias infusing her senses.

She was alone and it was relatively peaceful. The heavy curtains at the closed French doors managed to muffle the background bass still throbbing away inside. She could just make out the DJ whipping the party-goers into a pre-countdown frenzy as the hands of the clock inched closer to midnight.

The doors opened and she turned to see Tom, his trusty torch and truck still in hand.

'Hailey!'

'Hey, Tom,' she said as the little boy wandered over. 'Did you lose your father again?'

'Nah, he's coming too.'

Hailey helped him up onto the stone seat beside her. It was one of several placed periodically along the perimeter of the railing. Tom ran his truck back and forth along the rail, making engine noises.

The little boy looked even paler in the moonlight. Unnaturally pale. 'Did you get the truck for Christmas?' she asked.

Tom nodded.

'It's a beauty.'

Tom shrugged. 'It's OK.'

Hailey laughed. 'Didn't you want a truck?'

He shook his head. 'I wanted a baby brother.'

'Ah.' Hailey smiled. 'I see.'

'Daddy said that Santa can't give noonan beans as presents.' Tom sighed. 'He said we needed a mummy for that.'

Hailey bit her lip to stop laughing again. Tom was looking at her solemnly, obviously taking the subject very seriously indeed. So, there wasn't a mother on the scene? 'Right, yes, that's true.'

'Are you a mummy, Hailey?'

Hailey felt the laughter die in her throat. Nearly. Close. She'd been so close. She shook her head and forced a smile to her lips.

Callum escaped towards the balcony gratefully, pushing through the throngs that had gathered around the dance floor. It was only a few minutes until the clock clicked over into the new year and he didn't want to spend it with a bunch of half-inebriated strangers, kissing each other. He wanted to spend it with Tom. There'd been a few times when he hadn't been sure if his son would even make another year—the fact that he had was definitely worth celebrating.

He opened the French doors slightly and halted abruptly, his hand still on the handle. Tom was conversing with the woman from earlier. *Hailey*. Tom had taken a real liking to her. Her laughter floated towards him and he found his gaze drifting over her form. It had done that a little too much already tonight but the moonlight was silhouetting her figure so perfectly it was practically impossible not to do so.

She was short, barely taller than Tom perched on the chair next to her. Heavy ringlets escaped from a pile of hair arranged decoratively on the top of her head, brushing her bare shoulders and spilling down her back. Her red ballgown, cinched in at the waist, emphasised its narrowness and the sultry curve of her hips.

Callum felt a tug in his chest, seeing their heads close together, watching his son smile up at the mysterious Hailey. Tom had been through so much in his six years the fact that he could still smile was a miracle. He remembered her protective arm around Tom earlier and felt oddly unsettled.

He pushed the door fully open. 'Here you are,' he said, moving onto the balcony. 'I'm sorry, I hope he's not bothering you again.' Callum drew level with Tom and put his arm around his son's shoulders. It was his job to protect Tom. *His* job. He'd been doing it solo for six years.

Hailey smiled at Tom's father, the moonlight complementing the planes and angles of his face. Hailey, well used to having to look up at people, found he redefined the phrase *to crane one's neck*—she felt like a dwarf beside him. His mouth drew her gaze. It would have looked perfectly at home on a statue—the lips full and perfectly formed.

'No, we were just discussing the pros and cons of little brothers. Weren't we, Tom?'

Callum groaned and ruffled Tom's hair. 'Don't encourage him, please.'

'Hailey hasn't got any brothers either, Daddy. But she's got two sisters and a growed-up nephew called David and a baby niece called Birdie, and she's gonna be an aunty again in the middle of the year.'

Callum found himself wondering why she didn't have a couple of kids of her own. The image of her hand reaching for Tom's revisited him. Surely a woman this gorgeous was well and truly spoken for? He noticed the absence of rings on her fingers. 'Birdie?'

'Bridie.' Hailey corrected Tom's error with a laugh.

'Ah. Tom still had problems with his pronunciation.'

'I noticed.' Hailey smiled. 'That's what I like about him the best,' she said, winking at Tom, and was rewarded with a giggle.

They were interrupted by the ballroom erupting into a raucous countdown. 'Sixty, fifty-nine, fifty-eight…'

'Is it nearly midnight o'clock, Daddy?' Tom asked.

Callum chuckled. 'Nearly.'

'Fifty-two, fifty-one, fifty…'

'You'd better get back in there,' Callum said, looking down into her face. The moonlight emphasised the cute spray of freckles across her nose, illuminating each and every one. 'Your partner is probably looking for you.'

'Oh, no.' Hailey shook her head. 'I'm here by myself.'

What the…? Why had she told him that?

'Forty-two, forty-one, forty…'

Interesting. 'Here, matey, I got you one of these,' Callum said, handing a party blower to a suddenly excited Tom, who was hopping from one foot to the other as the crowd continued to count down. 'When everyone shouts "Happy New Year", we'll blow them together, OK?'

'But what about Hailey, Daddy? She needs one too.'

'Oh, no.' Hailey shook her head, realising belatedly they probably didn't want an interloper. 'It's fine. I'll leave you guys to bring in the new year with father-son whistleblowing.'

'Thirty-seven, thirty-six, thirty-five…'

'No. Don't go, Hailey, wait. We have more at the table. I'll get you one,' Tom said, leaping down from the chair and racing back inside before Hailey could stop him.

She watched him go, the plea in his high boyish voice clawing at her gut and freezing the self-preservation streak that had urged her to leave. What was she doing? She wasn't supposed to be getting involved like this any more—particularly with strangers.

Still, she didn't want to go inside. She told herself it was because of all the midnight merriment that was about to erupt. It was easier than thinking it was about him. The man she was now alone with. The stranger with heat in his eyes.

'Twenty, nineteen, eighteen…'

Hailey glanced at him. He was looking down at her, his grey-eyed gaze compelling. Somewhere inside her head she knew she should get the hell off this balcony and leave this man with his motherless little boy and their story well alone. She didn't know what it was and she didn't want to. But she found herself mesmerised by his eyes. She could hear the unsteadiness of her breath.

'Ten, nine, eight…'

Her pulse pounded through her head. This was crazy, this unwanted, almost electric attraction. It couldn't be happening. And yet it was. How could a complete stranger be so utterly fascinating?

'Three, two, one. Happy New Year!'

The ballroom erupted on a surge of cheers, breaking their intense connection. Hailey dragged her eyes away; her gaze, coming to rest on the mass of noonan beans, as Tom would call them, visible through the French doors. There was much hugging and kissing as 'Auld Lang Syne' was played.

She envied them their carefree revelry. She felt like she'd aged a couple of decades this last eighteen months, her previous flibbertigibbet existence blown to the four winds. And now this. A totally unexpected reaction to a perfect stranger. Even now, desperately concentrating on the crowd through the doors, she could feel his scrutiny. The heat emanating from his tall, tuxedo'd frame.

Hailey slowly became aware of the intimacy of some of the clinches. The couple closest to them hadn't come up for air since the countdown had hit zero and she looked away, embarrassed to be staring at their uninhibited display.

Callum coughed, also uncomfortable to be witnessing the couple's unbridled passion. 'Maybe they should get a room?'

Hailey looked up at him to agree and then wished she hadn't. He truly took her breath away. She stared at him again, helpless not to.

Callum sucked in a breath. The moonlight bathed her face, danced in her hair, washed over her bare neck and shoulders, throwing her cleavage into shadow and making it infinitely more mysterious, infinitely more fascinating.

'Happy New Year, Hailey.' His voice was husky and he mentally cursed at how tremulous it sounded.

'Happy New Year…'

She realised she didn't know his name. She thought about asking him but his gaze was on her mouth and her brain seemed more interested in that. And, anyway, not knowing his name gave her a distance from him she desperately needed.

Callum stared at her lips, plump and moist in the moonlight. He couldn't remember wanting to kiss anyone this badly in a very long time. He reached for her, placing his hand on her waist just where it flared into her hip and then leaned down, easing slowly towards her. Her eyelids had fluttered closed and he stopped just shy of her mouth as one lonely but very loud brain cell fought for control.

If he kissed her mouth, could he stop? It had been a long time and he already felt inexplicably, strangely drawn to this woman. He hadn't come here looking for this. And he certainly didn't need it. Tom was probably on his way back to them right now. He closed his eyes, changing direction subtly and dropped a soft kiss just beside her mouth.

It lingered. He didn't mean it to but it did anyway, taking on a life of its own, ignoring all sense. He pulled away, dazed by how something so chaste could be having such an effect on his body.

Hailey raised her hand to the spot where his mouth had seared her skin. She blinked, staring up at him for a long moment. His lips looked like they'd been carved by Michelangelo. She looked away, her gaze falling on the young couple closest to the French doors, still attached at the lips.

Hailey dropped her hand, suddenly tantalised by the idea of a full-on kiss with Tom's father. If a peck on the cheek could send her into such a spin, what havoc would the touch of his lips on hers create?

The doors were pushed open and Tom came bursting through them. 'I found one!'

They both stared at Tom, who was waving a party blower in front of them. Neither of them said a thing for a few seconds. Callum recovered first, taking a step back, his hand falling away from her waist.

Callum held out his arms and Tom ran into them gleefully. He swung him up high in the air. 'Happy New Year, Tommy.'

Tom giggled, hanging on tightly to his father's neck. 'Happy New Year, Daddy.'

Hailey laughed at them, an automatic reaction as her sluggish brain grappled with the surge of lust that had hijacked her body.

'This is for you, Hailey,' Tom said, handing her the whistle.

Hailey took it automatically. And joined in as Tom and his father blew their whistles at each other. Tom took great delight in hitting his father in the nose as the blower unravelled. Callum threw back his head and yelled, 'Happy New Year' at the moon, and Tom laughed, clinging to his father's neck, blowing his whistle at the stars.

Their merriment brought Hailey slowly out of her daze and she finally got into the spirit of the occasion, giving in to her inner child and also yelling at the heavens. Her heart squeezed painfully as she watched father and son dancing around the balcony. They were obviously very close and she felt the dormant bruise deep inside ache as if someone had prodded it.

Callum pulled up beside her, giving her a wink because kissing her again was out of the question. 'OK, Tom, time to go, it's way past your bedtime.'

'Oh, but, Dad, we're having so much fun,' Tom pleaded, blowing his whistle again for good measure.

'No "oh, buts", Callum growled playfully. 'I let you stay up to see in the new year because I promised…' He faltered as a memory of Tom last New Year's Eve, desperately ill in hospital, sent an itch up his spine. He cleared his throat. 'But now its bedtime for you. Say goodbye and thank you to Hailey for putting up with us.'

'Thanks Hailey. It was so-o-o much fun.'

'Yes, it was.' Hailey laughed and held out her hand. 'It was very nice meeting you.'

Tom shook it solemnly and Hailey smiled as he gave a very big yawn for a little boy. He snuggled his head into his father's chest and Hailey found herself wishing she could too. ''Night, sleepyhead.'

'Thanks,' Callum said to Hailey in a low voice. 'You were great with him.'

She shrugged casually as her pulse pounded through her head. 'He's a great kid.'

Callum looked down at his son's head, covered in sandy hair. 'Yes. He is.' He smiled at her again, before turning away from temptation and taking his leave.

Hailey stared at the French doors for a long while after they'd gone feeling curiously deflated. She could still feel the imprint of his lips on her cheek, the pull of her attraction to him. She turned away, facing the view, forcing herself to forget him. Forget the kiss.

But she couldn't deny how wonderful it felt as she stared blindly at the moon-kissed gardens below. Wonderful also to have a reprieve from the darker thoughts that had dogged her earlier. She'd tried really hard since her return not to indulge in self-pity. To be her usual, upbeat self. Her time on the balcony with Tom's father had certainly wiped out all thoughts of anything else.

It was rather freeing and she began to believe that there was going to be a time when what had happened in London would be completely behind her.

Her hand gripped the railing hard. *Bad idea, Hails. Very, very bad idea.*

She would not try to erase the memory of one man and his son by replacing them with another.

No matter how well the man could kiss.

CHAPTER TWO

'So?'

'So what?' Hailey fobbed off her sister.

'You disappeared out onto the balcony the other night. Did you find someone to bring in the new year with?' Rilla repeated with an exaggerated slowness.

'I'm really very busy, Ril,' Hailey said, avoiding the question again. She indicated the pile of charts she was working on. 'See these? See that sign?' She pointed to the sign on the wall near the light switch, 'It says Ward 2B. This is a hospital, remember.'

'So you did meet someone.' Rilla nodded sagely as she bit into her apple.

Hailey sighed in exasperation and threw down her pen. 'Isn't it busy down in Emergency? Don't you have a bus crash or something to be getting back to?'

'I'm on my break. Anyway, we're in a lull. They know I'm up here, visiting you, if they need me.'

Hailey knew she wasn't going to shake her sister. 'You know, just because you and Luca finally got your act together, it doesn't mean the rest of the world is looking for love.'

Rilla laughed. 'Hah! I knew it! What's his name?'

Hailey wished she could share that particular piece of

information with her sister but she hadn't found out her mystery kisser's name. Deliberately. She sighed, knowing capitulation was easier than trying to wrestle the bone from her sister. 'Tom's father?' she offered dubiously.

Rilla frowned. 'Tom? The kid with the truck?' She thought a bit more. 'Ah,' she said, realisation dawning, 'the military-looking dude? Mr Tuxedo?'

Hailey smiled at Rilla's nickname. Hadn't she been enthralled by how well he wore a suit? She filled her sister in on her balcony tryst, heavy on the detail with Tom, more hazy about his father.

'Oh, Hails. Do you think it's wise to get involved with another motherless boy?' Rilla asked gently.

Hailey hadn't told them much about what had happened in London but Rilla had known, they'd all known, that the sudden death of her sister's young charge had been a devastating blow. One thing was for sure, Hailey was certainly a very different person from the excitable young gadabout she'd been before her travels.

'I'm not involved,' Hailey denied hotly, despite three nights' worth of steamy dreams over a very non-steamy kiss. 'I'm never likely to come across them again. I don't even know who he is, for crying out loud.'

'Yes, but he was at the hospital ball so he must at least work here.'

Hailey shrugged. 'If he does, he's new. I'd never seen him before.' Someone that good-looking would certainly have stood out or at least been worthy of comment on the hospital grapevine.

'No, neither had I. Beth didn't know him either. I'll put some feelers out.'

Hailey rolled her eyes. 'Don't do it on my account.' As

her sister had so aptly pointed out, the very last thing she wanted in her life was another little boy. Or his father. 'How's the bump going?' she asked Rilla, deftly changing the subject.

They chatted for another fifteen minutes. Hailey listened half-heartedly to Rilla's baby prattle, her mind wandering again to Saturday night.

'I'll see you later. I'll ring if I find out anything about Mr Tuxedo.' Rilla winked as she departed.

'Great,' Hailey said brightly. Just what she needed, Rilla in matchmaker mode.

But her mind turned quickly to more pressing matters. This afternoon's meet and greet with the new director of paediatric services at the Brisbane General was a pretty big deal. She steeled herself mentally. The last director had been in his sixties and around for ever, and a real honey to boot. It had been sad to see him go.

Getting used to someone new was always a little fraught. Drastic changes to set practices often caused consternation and Hailey knew she wasn't the only member of staff who was nervous. She crossed her fingers that the transition wouldn't be too bumpy.

Hailey answered the phone in the nurses' station just before lunch. It was the lab with some renal function results and she dutifully wrote them down.

'Excuse me.'

'One moment,' Hailey said, not bothering to look up from the piece of paper as she double-checked the numbers.

'Thanks, George,' she said, replacing the phone, then scribbled the patient details down. 'Yes, sir, can I help you?'

Hailey looked up expectantly, her greeting dying on her

lips. Tom's father stood before her. He wore a pale lemon business shirt and a funky tie with polka-dot pigs emblazoned on it. He had a hospital ID with a smiley face sticker stuck over his face and a stethoscope slung around his neck.

'Tom's father,' she said absently.

Callum would have laughed had he not also been a little stunned from this development. Hailey was a nurse? Who worked on the kids' ward? Hailey, who had been on his mind a little too frequently the last few days. Hailey, who Tom had constantly chatted about—nothing but Hailey this and Hailey that since the ball.

She was in the standard uniform of plain navy pants and white shirt with the Brisbane General logo. Her hair was swept back into a no-nonsense ponytail complete with those familiar escaping tendrils brushing her neck.

'Callum. Callum Craig,' he supplied, holding out his hand, realising that he hadn't introduced himself the other night.

She took his firm warm hand in a daze and was instantly transported back to the moment he'd kissed her, his lips burning a brand into her cheek, his hand on her hip. She searched through the fog of lust in her head—where had she heard that name before?

'Is everything all right? Tom OK?' She frowned. 'Oh, God, he's not sick is he?'

No. Not any more. 'He's fine. I'm just a little early for my appointment, I guess.'

'Oh, I see,' Hailey said, not seeing at all. 'Were you here to see Yvonne?' His name was familiar but her brain cells still weren't working properly. Perhaps the NUM had mentioned his visit to her earlier?

'Partly, yes. I came to meet everyone and have a poke around.'

Hailey felt her pulse pick up and start to thrum through the veins in her head. 'Meet everyone?' she practically squeaked, suddenly realising why his name was so familiar.

'Yes. I'm the new director. Looks like we're going to be working together.'

Hailey nodded dumbly. This was Dr Callum Craig? The stranger who had kissed her on a balcony on New Year's Eve?

Oh, hell! So much for never seeing him again. The man was practically her boss!

Hailey spent the next two days avoiding him. When he was on the ward, she made herself scarce. The panroom, not a particularly fascinating place to be at the best of times, was her number-one choice for rooms in which to hide. It was certainly an inspired one. She'd never met a doctor yet who was comfortable around a bedpan. It was the one room they avoided like the plague.

She may not have known Callum Craig for very long but she'd known him long enough to know that she'd never had such an instantaneous reaction to a man. And there'd been plenty to make comparisons with. Her twenties had been strewn with brief, fun relationships. Light flirtations that hadn't gone the distance. They'd burnt brightly with all the pop and sparkle of giddy newness but had fizzled out quickly. Rilla and Beth had teased her that she'd changed her boyfriends as frequently as her underwear.

But none of them had ever had such an impact on such a short acquaintance. Not even Paul. And they'd bored her so quickly too. They had been boys compared to Callum Craig. She doubted he had a boring bone in his body. In short, Callum Craig unsettled her. And that was to be avoided at all costs. She was moving on with her life—she didn't need to complicate it by reaching for another attainable man.

A fleeting moonlight kiss at midnight from a stranger was one thing. She could hug it close, daydream about it and bring it out at night to relive over and over in her sleep. But when that man was a colleague? She had learnt the hard way not to mix work with her private life. What had happened in London had burnt her so badly she was sworn off men for life.

Particularly men with little boys.

Callum entered the ward on Thursday afternoon to attend his ward round. He spotted Hailey just as she was disappearing into the panroom. Again.

She was avoiding him.

OK, he got it. Her signals were coming across loud and clear. *Back off. Not interested. Don't even think about it.*

She obviously regretted their midnight madness.

He wished the same could be said for him. It was, after all, the most sensible course of action. The very last thing he needed now was to develop a thing for a woman who wanted nothing to do with him.

His six years alone—coping with his wife's death and a six-month-old baby and then struggling to raise Tom and get him through his illness, scared to death most of the time—seemed suddenly magnified. Maybe that was what happened? Maybe Hailey's kiss had made him realise what a solitary life he led. Why else would his body be reacting so strongly to a woman who was so patently not interested?

Because he didn't have the time or the wherewithal for any kind of a relationship. He'd spent the last six years protecting Tom, shielding him from the things life had thrown at him—the loss of his mother and a truly vile illness. He'd dropped the ball with Annie, he wouldn't do the same with Tom.

But he didn't have time for this hide-and-seek routine either. They were both adults and this state of affairs couldn't continue. She couldn't keep avoiding him for ever. They had to work together. They were two mature adults. Surely they could act that way?

He glanced at his watch. Five minutes before Yvonne was expecting him for rounds. He took a moment to collect his thoughts and pushed open the panroom door.

'Afternoon, Hailey.'

Hailey started. She had her back to the door, checking the expiry dates on the various test sticks that were kept in the wall cupboard above the sink. Over the last few days she'd done a pretty decent inventory of the room's contents. She turned around slowly, her heart rate tripping from a surge of adrenaline.

He looked divine. His stethoscope was slung casually around his neck and his shirt fitted his broad-shouldered frame to perfection. His tie today sported leaping leprechauns and his smile exuded charisma. She felt his pull despite the good three metres between them. 'I think you took a wrong turn. Yvonne's office is two doors down.'

Callum's smile widened. 'Nope. This is the right door. I was after you.'

Her heart slammed in her chest. 'Me?' she practically squeaked.

'You've been kind of hard to pin down these last few days.'

'Ah, yes...' she said nervously. She dragged in a ragged breath, feeling like all the oxygen was being sucked out of the room. 'A nurse's work is never done,' she said lamely, shaking the bottle of urine sticks, which she hadn't realised she was holding, in his general direction.

'Are you in Yvonne's bad books? Have you been banished to the panroom for the term of your natural life?'

'Er…no,' she said, her dazzled brain cells trying to keep track of the conversation.

'Ah. So you're just avoiding me?'

Bingo! Hailey stared at him for a moment before turning back to the cupboard, horrified at the rise of heat in her cheeks. 'Don't be ridiculous.' Her hand shook as she replaced the container.

Callum watched her as her fingers ran over the contents of the cupboard. 'Hailey.' Her fingers stilled but she didn't answer him. 'Hailey,' he said again, moving closer.

Hailey turned around reluctantly and then immediately wished she hadn't. He loomed in front of her and she was reminded of the ball all over again as she looked all the way up into his face. His very sexy face. If she'd thought his pull had been strong from across the room, it was nothing compared to his power close up.

'God, you're tiny,' Callum said, distracted by their height disparity. Maybe it had been the moonlight but he didn't remember her being so far down.

Hailey snorted. 'No, I'm short. There's a difference.' She had lost weight over the last year, the effects of what had happened overseas shadowing all areas of her life. But Hailey doubted that her generous curves were under any real threat of fading away.

'How tall are you?'

'Five foot neat.'

No wonder he felt like he was towering over her. At

four inches over six feet—he did! He kind of liked it, though. It made him want to tuck her under his wing. 'Wow. That is short.'

Hailey's breath caught at his light teasing tone and the smile that took his features from sexy to the next level. Whatever the hell that was. Sublime? 'Don't let it fool you. I came top in my self-defence class.'

Callum laughed. 'Really?'

Hailey drew herself up as high as she could and jutted her chin out. 'Really.'

Callum quashed his smile. 'I'll have to remember that.'

Hailey placed a hand on his chest and pushed him gently away until he was a full arm's length from her. 'Just you see that you do.'

Callum saw the look of steel harden her soft brown eyes. 'Look, Hailey, I'm guessing the whole New Year's Eve thing is kind of freaking you out. I'm sorry. I promise I don't usually go around kissing women I don't know.' Hell, these days he just didn't kiss women—period.

Sorry? He was sorry? For what? For freaking her out or kissing her in the first place? She shouldn't feel miffed. But she did. 'You're apologising for kissing me?' *Good. That was good. Wasn't it?*

'No. Absolutely not.' The actual kiss may have been no more than a peck but the way it was still zinging through his body it may as well have been a full-on, open-mouthed smacker. Callum hadn't felt such ardent desire since Annie. It felt good to have that rush again. That buzz in his blood. He certainly wasn't going to apoligise for it. 'I'd do it again. No hesitation.'

She swallowed. 'Oh.'

Of course he hadn't meant right now but her lips had

parted on that last word and her face was turned up, her mouth looking very inviting indeed. What would it be like to indulge in more than a chaste, oh-so-close-to-her-mouth kiss?

He took a step back. They were in a panroom, for crying out loud! At work! He cleared his throat. 'Anyway. My point is…' he said, groping around his brain for the point he was trying to articulate. 'The point is, it happened. I don't think we need to let it affect our working together. Let's just chalk it up to a bit of moonlight madness and get on with it. OK? I don't want you ducking in and out of rooms, avoiding me, ad infinitum. It won't happen again.'

'You just said you'd do it again,' she pointed out, her brain still stuck back at that part of the conversation.

'I meant that night. I'd do it all over again the same way. I couldn't think of a better ending to a New Year's Eve ball than kissing a girl with sparkly legs.'

Hailey smiled despite her mind still being foggy with his nearness. 'It can't happen again,' she said firmly.

Callum frowned. 'You didn't like it?'

'No, I…'

He smiled. 'Ah. You did like it?'

Hailey crossed her arms and gave him a hard glare. She barely knew him and yet already he could tie her in knots! 'Don't be putting words in my mouth, Dr Craig.'

'Ooh.' He laughed at her frown. 'You liked it a lot.'

Hailey felt her temper rise as heat flared in her cheeks again. She daren't admit just how much she had liked the brief touch of his mouth. 'It was a peck on the cheek,' she said disparagingly. 'My brother-in-law could have given it to me.'

Callum raised an eyebrow. 'Is that a challenge? Is that your way of asking for something…more?'

The remaining oxygen evaporated and her eyes were

drawn inexplicably to his mouth. More? How could something so wrong seem so...tantalising? A couple of years ago she'd have leapt at him. That mouth would have been on hers in a flash. But she just wasn't that girl any more.

'You need to get this straight,' she said, deliberately dragging her eyes away from his lips. 'I'm not in the market for a...an affair, and even if I was, which I'm not,' she emphasised again, 'I don't get involved with colleagues.'

Callum could see the determination in the jut of her chin and her steady brown gaze. He could also see something else. A quick flash of pain before she shuttered it. 'Is that a standard policy for you or a once-bitten kind of thing?'

Hailey's breath caught in her throat and her mind stuttered to a halt for a brief second. Had that been a wild guess or had she given something away? She forced herself to casually check her watch while she ordered her scattered thoughts. 'Don't you have rounds?'

Hmm. A chink. Hailey had definitely been burned. Big time if he wasn't mistaken. Callum regarded her for a few seconds. Well so had he and he wasn't keen to put himself in a position of vulnerability again either. He nodded. 'So we're OK now?'

Hailey nodded too. Anything to get him out of the room. It seemed to have shrunk considerably since he'd entered. 'Of course.'

'It's behind us?'

'Absolutely.'

'Forgotten?'

'There was no kiss.'

Callum smiled. 'Kiss? What kiss?'

Hailey smiled back at him. He touched his fingers to

his forehead in a mock salute as he slowly backed out of the room. She sagged against the sink. If only it was as easy as that.

The phone was ringing when Hailey ventured out of the panroom a few minutes later. Callum's team had gathered in the nurses' station. They were ignoring the phone. Tina, the ward clerk, had left for the day.

Hailey looked at the medical officers. Callum, a registrar, two residents and two med students. 'No, it's OK,' she said, half bemused, half annoyed. 'I'll get the phone.' It never ceased to amaze her how immune to ringing medical staff were.

'Hi, kids' ward, Hailey speaking.'

'Hi, Hailey.'

'Yvonne?' What was 2B's NUM doing, ringing her? She should be here.

'Can you do Callum's round? I'm caught up in this funding meeting and I need to stay because they're discussing our equipment allocation.'

Hailey sighed, resigned to her fate. She glanced at Callum and met his calm grey gaze. OK, she wasn't going to avoid him any more but that didn't mean she wanted to spend any extra time with him. 'Sure,' she said averting her gaze. 'Is Dad there?'

'He's chairing it.'

Hailey's father, John Winters, was the Brisbane General's medical director. He spent his entire day in meetings such as these. 'Blow him a kiss for me,' she said, then hung up the phone.

'Looks like you got me, folks,' she said, addressing the entourage. She risked another glance at Callum. A small smile was playing on that very fascinating mouth. 'Let's get this show on the road.'

2B was a twenty-bed ward. In an ideal world eight beds were allocated to surgical patients, eight to medical patients and four formed a high-dependency bay for those children that needed closer monitoring. Of course, the balance was often weighted more heavily one way or the other which caused all kinds of administration headaches.

But that was the nature of hospitals and as far as nursing their patients went, Hailey couldn't give a fig about the medical/surgical mix—they were all sick kids.

She pushed the chart trolley from bed to bed as each patient and their progress was discussed. She hadn't done a round with Callum before and was most impressed with his unique mix of professionalism, thoroughness and quirky bedside manner. He developed a quick rapport with the parents and wasn't afraid to take the time with the kids to touch them and try and elicit a smile or two.

Hailey had been on too many ward rounds that were rushed and left the parents with more questions than answers. Callum didn't operate that way. He seemed genuinely interested, concerned and willing to listen. He also engaged his entire team, med students included, teaching as he went, and it was obvious they liked and respected him.

He was careful to include her as well, seeking her opinion, consulting her about decisions, making it nigh on impossible not to interact with him. She'd hoped the round would be quick and painless but she'd been wrong. She was more aware of him than ever now she'd seen the professional side of him.

The truth was, even after thirty minutes, she had to grudgingly admit she admired the hell out of him. An irresistible mix when the kiss-that-never-happened still loomed large in her consciousness. Damn it all. This was a man she could like.

The surgical bays were full of the morning's ENT list. Several tonsillectomies, some with adenoids as well and others with grommets. The surgeons would be in to see them later but Callum took the time to check all was well with them.

The medical bays sported a mix of conditions. From their frequent flyer, Lucy, with cystic fibrosis, to Troy, an eight-year-old cerebral palsy patient with pneumonia, and an adventurous three-year-old, Jake, who had petted a possum and ended up with a bitten arm for his trouble. The wound had developed cellulitis, necessitating intravenous antibiotics.

'Hello, Jake,' Callum greeted as they stopped at the three-year-old's bedside. 'I heard you wrestled a lion the other day.'

Jake giggled and looked at his mother, who smiled at Callum. 'No, it was a crocodile, wasn't it, Jakey?'

Jake giggled again.

'Is it OK if I have a look at where this croc got you?' Callum grinned.

Jake nodded shyly and held out his bandaged arm. The other arm was wrapped up too, to secure the IV. Hailey reached out to remove the dressing but Callum had already started unwinding it. She was so used to doing things like this for doctors that it was a nice change to come across one who could do his own dirty work.

'Ah, now, see here,' Callum said to his students as he revealed the wound. 'This is a classic case of cellulitis. A central wound and a reddened area of skin surrounding it where the subcutaneous tissues have been inflamed. And see,' Callum said, pointing to the perfectly formed outer edge of the angry-looking area, 'the definite demarcation line where the inflammation halts.'

The students peered closer and nodded.

'How big was that croc, Jake?' Callum asked. 'That's an impressive wound.'

'He was this big,' Jake said, his eyes almost as wide as his outstretched arm span, getting into the swing of the game.

The team laughed. Hailey was still smiling when Callum rewound the bandage. Their gazes met and Callum winked at her. Her smile slipped. The memory of how he had done exactly that on the balcony taunted her and the strange fluttery sensation it had caused in the pit of her stomach returned.

'He's going to need longer on the antibiotics,' Callum said, addressing Jake's mother. 'We'll review the wound every day but I wouldn't count on being out of here for at least two more days.'

The team waited for Callum to wash his hands and then moved on to the four-bedded high-dependency bay, directly opposite the nurses' station, which currently housed only three patients.

There was twelve-month-old Henry, an ex-prem baby with a trachy tube for his floppy airway. His mother usually managed him at home but Henry had developed a respiratory infection and had become quite sick very rapidly, ending up in ICU for a week. He was on the mend now and was due for discharge some time in the next few days.

In the next bed Tristan, a very healthy-looking four-year-old was sitting up, watching television with his father. He was being monitored after ingestion of four of his grandmother's blood-pressure tablets. He was in hospital as a precaution only and, barring any unexpected adverse reaction, would be discharged tomorrow.

Tahlia, a very cute newborn diabetic, was kicking up a ruckus. She'd also been a transfer from ICU. She would be with them for some time while her parents learned how to manage the condition.

'Can you hold her while I go and get her bottle?' Rosemary, the junior nurse who'd been allocated the bay for the shift, asked Hailey.

Hailey nodded and took the swaddled infant. Tahlia, well used to being picked up after her four weeks in hospital, settled instantly. Hailey held her while the round continued.

'You're a natural,' Callum murmured as he brushed past her to wash his hands.

Hailey looked down into Tahlia's blue gaze and realised she'd been subconsciously swaying. Well, yes, she was a paeds nurse after all. And prior to that she'd been a midwife. So, yes, she was good with kids.

But she wasn't the same nurse who had gone away to London. What had happened there had taught her to keep her emotional distance. Made her wary of getting too involved with her patients. Once she may have been a natural. Now she was just doing her job.

Rosemary came back and Hailey handed Tahlia over gratefully. The round ended and Hailey scurried away to let the other nurses know the relevant changes pertaining to their patients and then sat to document the decisions from the round in each patient's chart.

She was aware of Callum as his team lingered in the nurses' station. His voice was totally distracting, deep and well modulated—very easy on the ear. His laugh practically shimmied along her nerves, shattering her concentration.

They eventually took their leave. Callum said goodbye and she returned it, not looking up from the chart, feigning complete absorption in her task. But her hand shook betrayingly and she let out a breath as Callum, his voice and his laugh finally left the ward.

An hour later, Hailey was counting down the minutes to the end of her shift—ten, to be exact—and the start of her days off. She hadn't been able to stop thinking about Callum's comments and she was looking forward to having a few days' respite from his presence.

She was checking all her patient's fluid charts when Joyce, the ward cleaner, approached. Joyce had been cleaning 2B's floors and keeping everything spick and span for over two decades. Hailey had no doubt that at any given time she could eat off the floors safe in the knowledge that no bacteria would dare challenge the cleaner's authority. Joyce was almost part of the furniture around the ward and was regarded as one of the team.

There was an old adage in nursing. Patients told doctors a little, nurses a lot and the cleaning staff everything. And a good nurse knew it. Joyce was her first port of call when one of the parents was reticent with information.

'There's an alarm going off next door.' Joyce jabbed her thumb towards the high-dependency bay. 'There's no one in there.'

An urgent beeping from a saturation monitor worked its way into her consciousness. She realised then that it had been going off for a while. Hailey frowned. There was no one there? She'd subconsciously blocked the noise out, knowing it was Rosemary's bay and the other nurse was supposed to be there.

The alarm persisted and Hailey thanked Joyce, making her way next door. She didn't hurry, knowing that it would probably be just a dislodged probe. The bay was empty of any parents and also empty of Rosemary, as Joyce had indicated. She wasn't supposed to leave the high-dependency bay without getting someone to take her place. The alarm was coming from Henry's bed and Hailey strolled over, still unconcerned.

But when she got there, it was immediately obvious the alarm was for real. The sats monitor was recording Henry's oxygen saturations as seventy per cent and one look at Henry confirmed the dire figure. He was flailing his arms around, gasping for air, like a fish out of water, his lips and peripheries tinged with blue, sweat beading his forehead.

'Oh, no,' Hailey muttered. Was Henry's trachy blocked or had he just worked himself into a state, exacerbating his malacia? She hit the emergency call button on the wall near the end of the cot with one hand as she manoeuvred the cot side down with the other.

Callum, who had returned to the ward to fill out the paperwork for a pending admission, was at the nurses' station when the distinctive tone of the emergency call went off. He looked at the nurse call board that displayed all the bed numbers and quickly located the source of the emergency.

He strode into the high-dependency bay to find a very worried Hailey frantically suctioning Henry's trachy. One look at the little boy's panic-filled gaze and cyanosed lips was enough to confirm the urgency of the situation.

'What happened?' he demanded, yanking the resus bag off the wall and twisting on the oxygen meter it was connected to, satisfied to hear the hiss of gas inflating the bag.

'Not sure. I think he must have plugged his trachy,'

Hailey said, withdrawing the suction catheter from the artificial airway. 'It's no use. I can't pass it. It must be completely blocked.'

Callum nodded, trusting her assessment. 'We're going to have to replace it.'

The alarm continued to trill in the background, the tone getting lower as Henry's saturations continued to plummet further. Fifty, forty-nine, forty-eight. The little boy's colour was getting worse the more oxygen deprived he became.

Hailey glanced at Callum, her heartbeat thundering in her ears. A red flush was creeping up her neck. She hesitated a split second before she nodded.

'What's the matter?' Yvonne demanded as two other nurses, including a very pale-looking Rosemary, joined them.

'Get the resus trolley,' Hailey ordered, her gaze not leaving her patient as she fumbled with the emergency box of supplies kept on Henry's bedside cabinet.

'I'll dilate the stoma,' Callum said as he snipped the tapes that secured the useless trachy in place. 'You place the airway.'

Hailey nodded as she handed him the trachy dilators. The noise of the alarm and the controlled panic that surrounded her as Yvonne barked orders and nurses performed their much practised roles faded as adrenaline honed her instincts. She was aware only of Callum and Henry as they worked in tandem to secure the little boy a patent airway.

Callum whipped out the old trachy and inserted the dilators into the hole in Henry's neck. Hailey, her fingers trembling, ripped open the packaging of a new trachy and deftly inserted the sturdy, plastic airway into the tract. She held it in place for Callum as he attached the resus bag and gently puffed some breaths into Henry's lungs.

The little boy pinked up almost immediately, the tone on the sats monitor getting higher and higher as his oxygen saturations climbed rapidly back into the nineties. Henry started to cry as panic was replaced with relief. The whole episode had obviously terrified him.

'Crisis averted,' Callum said, letting out a pent-up breath.

Hailey nodded. It had seemed like an hour, though, in reality, only two minutes had passed since Joyce had alerted her to the emergency. But their job wasn't over yet and she wasn't going to break out the champagne until it was. 'Let's secure it,' she said.

Despite not being able to make any noise due to the position of the trachy, Henry was still bawling, great silent sobs, taking full advantage of being able to fill his lungs with air.

'It's OK, baby,' Hailey murmured as she tied the trachy tapes, anchoring them around the back of his neck. It was a finicky job at the best of times, made that much more difficult by an aggrieved Henry and her badly trembling fingers.

Henry's crying was exacerbated by frequent coughing bouts and by the time the tapes were tied and Hailey had suctioned him, the little boy was in a state. Hailey didn't give it a second thought. She scooped the little boy up into her arms and hugged him tightly to her.

'Shh, baby, shh,' she crooned, rocking him, her own heart rate galloping as she allowed herself to think about the potential consequences had she not responded to Joyce's comment.

Callum put a hand on her shoulder and one on Henry's back, rubbing it gently, also murmuring soothing words to the fractious child. Hailey didn't object, too pleased to have had Callum with her during the incident to reject his company now.

She could hear Yvonne talking to Rosemary about the importance of vigilance somewhere behind her. Henry was settling and she pressed her forehead against his, shutting her eyes.

'You OK?'

Hailey looked up into Callum's concerned grey gaze. She gave a half laugh, half sigh. 'I am now.'

Callum smiled. He was seeing a different side to Hailey. She was holding Henry tightly reminding him of a mother lion with one of her cubs. Like the way she'd drawn Tom close the other night. He'd been right earlier—she was a natural. She'd known instinctively that Henry had needed comfort. Just as she had known how to talk to Tom the other night. Not like a bratty, unwelcome kid, but like an equal.

'Thank you. You were great.'

'Really?' She grimaced. 'I felt all fingers and thumbs.'

He nodded, still stroking Henry's back. 'You were very cool under pressure.'

She did laugh this time. 'Didn't feel very cool inside.'

He shrugged. 'That's only normal. We wouldn't be human if something like this didn't freak us out a little.'

Hailey rubbed her cheek against Henry's head as he snuggled into her neck. 'You, too?'

'Just because I wear a white coat, it doesn't mean that an emergency situation won't send my blood pressure up.'

Hailey nodded. She'd dealt with quite a few emergency situations over the course of her nursing career but they still managed to turn her into jelly on the inside. It was nice to hear an experienced paediatrician admitting to similar feelings.

'He's asleep.'

Hailey looked down into Henry's sweet, sleeping face. 'I'm sure he's utterly exhausted, poor darling.' She laid him gently back in his cot.

Callum watched as she covered him with a colourful bunny rug and lingered, caressing his cheek. She obviously cared about her young charges. She would make a great mother. The kind of mother Tom had been nagging him about to give him that baby brother.

'I'd better get back to my paperwork,' he said, dragging his thoughts away from the realm of fantasy.

Hailey watched him go, her hand still on the sleeping bundle in the cot. Working side by side with Callum to bring Henry back from the brink had been real nail-biting stuff but she couldn't deny how alive it had made her feel or how long it had been since she'd felt this invigorated.

It would be wrong to read too much into it.

CHAPTER THREE

THE buzz that had infused Hailey immediately after the emergency with Henry dissipated quickly and she left the hospital feeling edgy. Coming down from an adrenaline rush always left her with a jittery, strung-out feeling. The best antidote for that? Shopping.

She drove to her apartment and had a quick shower, pleased to be rid of her uniform. She'd always worn it with pride but some days it was too much a reminder of work and her hand trembled slightly as she remembered the events of the day. She wished she could be sure it was the effects of the adrenaline but she suspected Callum's touch, as she had held Henry, was also having an impact.

Damn the man. Things were finally getting back on track in her life. She didn't need to derail her progress like this. She threw on some clothes, picked up her bag and strode out of her apartment, determined not to think about work or Henry's blue lips and panicked face or Callum Craig.

The noise of the crowds and the hustle and bustle were instantly distracting. The announcements over the PA and the piped music gave her something else to think about. The concentration required to calculate discounts and specials and colour co-ordinate with her existing wardrobe was wonderfully absorbing. OK, her local shopping mall was hardly Oxford Street but it was good therapy nevertheless.

Yes, there were probably healthier ways of dealing with work stress. Fitness freaks probably would have jogged it out of their system. Or gone to the gym. Or to their favourite health-food bar and overdosed on carrot juice and wheatgrass smoothies.

Or some may even have rung a close work colleague or their best friend and debriefed. Gone out for a drink. Shot the breeze. Sought some female comfort. But Hailey had felt too disconnected from her friends since her return from overseas to have even considered that option.

Still, shopping was better than some pursuits. A nurse she'd befriended in London used to go out to a nightclub and pick up a man after a particularly harrowing shift. She'd maintained that there was nothing like sex to make you forget. And perhaps she'd been right. But Hailey was hard pressed at the moment not to think of sex and Callum Craig together so that definitely hadn't been an option.

Hailey's mobile rang while she was in a fitting room. It was Rilla.

'Hello?' she murmured in a low voice, not wanting every other customer in the change rooms to be privy to her conversation.

'Hailey? Is that you?'

'Yes,' she murmured again.

'Why are you whispering? I can barely hear you.'

'I'm not whispering!' she muttered crankily. 'I'm kind of occupied right now. What do you want?'

'Beth and I are coming over. We'll be there about seven. Don't cook—we'll bring food.'

'Rilla.' Hailey shook her head. Her sisters must have heard

about Henry. One disadvantage to having your entire family working in the same medical facility. 'There's no need.'

'Yes. There is. See you later.'

Hailey stared at the dead phone. She looked at her watch. Five-thirty! An hour and a half, and the apartment was a mess. She wriggled out of the jeans she was trying on and dressed quickly.

Peak-hour traffic was the pits and she tapped impatiently on the steering-wheel as her time narrowed further. She screeched into her parking space with less than thirty minutes to spare. She loaded herself up with her parcels, shunning the often slow lifts and thinking of how great seven flights of stairs would be for her butt and calves. If they didn't kill her first.

She took them steadily, pleased to realise her afternoon of shopping and the mad dash home had left her no time to think about the way her shift had ended. Or Callum Craig either, for that matter. Not his quiet confidence in the face of a crisis or his hand on her shoulder, asking her if she was OK.

Although his wicked wink during the ward round did rear its head at her as she dashed up the last ten steps, her thighs screaming in protest. Her foot faltered briefly as she thought about his panroom visit. In that split second, distracted by the memory, she misjudged the tread and stumbled, pitching forward, her ankle twisting as she landed unceremoniously in a crumpled heap, her parcels covering her, half spilling their contents over the hallway.

Hailey cried out as a stabbing pain tore through her ankle and she shut her eyes against the quick sting of tears that filled her vision.

'Are you all right?'

She kept her eyes shut, ignoring the concerned male voice as the pain gripped relentlessly. She nodded, holding her breath, biting her lip against the very unladylike oath on the tip of her tongue. *Did she look all right sprawled on the floor like this?*

'Will she be OK, Daddy?'

Hailey's eyes shot open, the pain temporarily overridden. It couldn't be. Tom stared down at her. She blinked. Callum was kneeling on the floor beside her, his worried face peering down into hers. Suddenly, despite the pain slowly releasing her from its grip, things just got a whole lot worse.

'What are you doing here?' It slipped out before she could stop it but honestly! *Was he stalking her?*

Callum frowned. 'Hailey?'

'Hailey!' Tom grinned, waving at her frantically.

Tom's waggling fingers were nauseating from that angle so she moved gingerly, rising up onto her elbows, wincing as pain clawed at her ankle again.

'Don't move,' Callum ordered, placing a stilling hand on her shoulder. 'You may have injured your neck.'

'I did not injure my neck,' she grouched. *Just my pride.* 'I hurt my ankle, that's all.'

Tom knelt beside her too, mimicking his father. She noted his torch firmly ensconced under his arm. He placed a hand on her arm. 'My daddy's a doctor,' he said solemnly. 'Better do as he says.'

She looked at Callum, who was having trouble suppressing a smile. 'Over my dead body,' she muttered under her breath, levering herself into a sitting position. She reached for the closest article of clothing that lay strewn on the carpet and plucked it up, shoving it back in a bag.

'Here, let me help you,' Callum said, also reaching for

the spilled contents. His hand fell on a black lace bra and
knicker set. The fabric felt cool beneath his touch and he
couldn't help but wonder how it would look adorning her
as he passed it to her.

Hailey met his gaze and saw the flare of heat in his eyes.
She snatched it from him, annoyed at the tremor of lust that
coursed through her body just like the night on the balcony.
'I can manage, thank you,' she said primly.

She gathered the stuff quickly, very aware of Callum
and Tom watching her. 'What are you doing here anyway?'
She repeated her unanswered question from earlier as she
shoved the last garment back into its bag.

'I live here,' Callum stated. 'Three doors down.'

Hailey looked at him sharply. He *lived* here? Was there
some conspiracy out there that she didn't know about?
'I've never seen you here before.' Not that she was that up
to date on the comings and goings in the complex. Shift
work made it difficult to keep tabs on anything. 'When did
you move in?'

'Two weeks ago.'

Two weeks? They'd been here for a fortnight? She
searched back in her mind. She'd been on a run of nights then.

'What are you doing here? Are you visiting someone?'

Callum's question cut into her thoughts. 'I live here,
too,' she said miserably. She pointed to her door three
down in the opposite direction.

Callum looked at the door, the full implications
dawning. 'So we're neighbours?'

'It would appear so,' Hailey admitted, her heart beating
a little too fast at the thought.

'Oh, goody, Daddy. Hooray! Hailey is our neighbour!'

Tom jumped up and down excitedly while Callum tried

not to think about black lace underwear. She looked sexy enough in her strappy, clingy sundress. The last thing he wanted was temptation living down the corridor.

They looked at each other for a few moments, both unhappy about the unexpected development. Hailey broke eye contact first.

'Anyway, sorry to have intruded on your day. I'll be going now.' She grabbed the railing and hoisted herself into a standing position, gritting her teeth at the jab of pain.

'Whoa,' Callum chided as Hailey swayed and he placed a steadying hand on her shoulder. 'Careful. Let me help you.'

'I'm fine,' she said, ignoring the proffered arm and gingerly putting her sore foot to the floor. It was probably only ten metres to her door but it suddenly seemed ten kilometres as her ankle protested the movement.

Callum rolled his eyes at the obvious wince on Hailey's face. 'Lean on me,' he ordered, putting an arm around her waist.

'I'm fine,' she reiterated, even though she knew it was going to take some time to cover the distance.

'Or I could pick you up,' Callum said, exasperated. 'Your choice.'

'You'd better be prepared to get your fingers broken if you do,' she threatened, looking all the way up into his face.

'Taught you that in your self-defence class too, huh?'

She nodded. 'That, and how to break planks with my bare hands.'

Callum threw back his head and laughed. 'I'll bear that in mind. Come on, just lean on me. Think of it as neighbourly.'

Except it didn't feel neighbourly as she acquiesced. She was excruciatingly aware of the rub of his hip against her side, the brush of his arm around her waist. It even managed to obliterate the slow, steady throb in her ankle.

Tom followed them, laden with the shopping bags, and Hailey's handbag. He fished through it for Hailey's keys and passed them to his father. Within a minute Hailey was ensconced on her lounge.

'Thank you,' she said, looking up at Callum. From her reclining position he looked even further up. He was wearing his work clothes but his tie had been removed and his top buttons undone and his sleeves rolled up to his elbow. He looked relaxed and utterly at home in her unit.

Leave now.

'Have you got a first-aid kit? I'll strap it. And put ice on it. That should reduce the swelling. What about pain-killers? I have some at my place if you haven't got anything.'

'That won't be necessary,' Hailey dismissed, smiling at Tom as he shone his torch on the inflammation around her ankle. It didn't look too awful and the pain had settled to a dull throb. It didn't look like a bad sprain.

Leave now.

But Callum was already poking around in her kitchen, opening her freezer, helping himself to its contents.

'Here, we'll use this,' Callum said, brandishing a bag of frozen veg. 'Tom, can you grab those cushions off the other lounges?' he asked as he knelt down and moulded the freezing cold bag to the contours of her ankle.

Hailey opened her mouth to protest but his fingers felt gentle against her throbbing joint and she knew it needed ice. She winced as the cold enveloped her inflamed joint. Tom helped Callum lift her foot and settle it on top of a pile of cushions.

'R.I.C.E.,' Callum said, satisfied. 'Rest, ice, compression and elevation. I'll leave that on for about ten minutes and then strap it for you. Do you have some paracetamol?'

He was looking at her and his hand was on her shin, shooting heat right up to her thigh. In her mind's eye she could see him running it up higher, under the hem of her dress. Higher.

Leave now.

'That's really not necessary,' she said. 'You've done more than enough and—'

'Hailey!' Callum interrupted. What was it with women these days? Why didn't they want a man to take care of them? Annie had been like that. 'I'm a doctor. I'm not leaving here until your ankle's strapped and I've got you something to dull the pain. It's the least I can do. So just tell me where the damn painkillers are.'

Hailey blinked at Callum's exasperated tone. She looked at Tom. Tom looked at Hailey. 'Bathroom cupboard,' she sighed.

'Boy,' Tom said in awe. 'You made my daddy really cranky.'

'Doesn't he get cranky usually?'

Tom thought about it. 'Only with Grandma sometimes.'

'Oh?'

'She doesn't think I should do stuff like climb trees.'

'Oh, I see,' Hailey said, not really seeing at all.

Callum strode back into the lounge room, a glass of water and a packet of pills in his hand. 'Take these.'

His voice brooked no argument and Hailey swallowed two, knowing that the less it hurt, the more she'd be able to gently exercise it, the quicker it would recover.

'Bandage?' he asked.

Hailey didn't bother with protesting. The sooner he did

what he felt was his professional duty, the sooner he could leave. 'First-aid box under the sink.'

She returned her gaze to Tom, who gave her a grin. 'You like television?' she asked. 'I have cable.'

Tom nodded enthusiastically and she got him to pass her the remote control and she surfed until she found a suitable kids' show.

Callum returned and knelt by her foot again. He lifted the frozen veg away and inspected the swelling. 'It doesn't look too serious,' he mused, prodding gently, and proceeded to wrap it firmly.

The feel of her cool skin beneath his fingers was stupidly sensual. He blinked. 'Nice place you have here.' Not that he'd noticed a damn thing about it as having her body pressed against his on the way in had totally removed all his cognitive powers.

'Er, yes,' she said, gathering her wits. The light slide of his fingers as he wound the bandage around her ankle feathered her skin with goose-bumps. 'It's Rilla's. My sister. She bought it after her separation from Luca but now they're back together again and I needed to be on my own and Beth, my other sister, suggested I rent it so it worked out quite well really.'

Callum's fingers stilled. She'd needed to be on her own? *Intriguing.* He'd known something wasn't right with her.

'There's a great view of the river and it's so close to everything.'

Of course, he would know that, given that he lived here as well. Shut up, damn it! She was babbling. But, honestly, how could something as asexual as applying a bandage to a disgustingly puffy ankle be so erotic?

Callum nodded absently, searching for a topic that

would distract him from the insane urge to bend his head to her injury and a drop a kiss against it. He'd been a dad for too long. Hell, he'd been single too long.

'I'm glad I got a chance to see you again today, actually. I wanted to check if you were OK this afternoon but you'd already left.'

The touch of his hand was terribly distracting and she frowned at him, trying to make sense of what he'd said. 'OK?'

'The thing with Henry...' he prompted.

'Hmm? Oh, right. Sure, sure.' She nodded her head for proper emphasis and pointed to the discarded shopping bags. 'Retail therapy. Works every time. You?' she asked.

He lifted his gaze to her face and shrugged. 'Tom is a pretty good antidote to most things.'

Tom chose that moment to giggle at something funny on television and they both glanced at him and smiled. 'Yeah, I bet he is,' she said softly.

Callum heard the wistful note in her voice and glanced back at her sharply. Her voice was pregnant with longing yet her eyes seemed muddied with confusion. 'Family's good for that,' he murmured gently.

Hailey flicked her gaze back to Callum, aware again of his hand on her leg. This had to stop. 'Speaking of which, my sisters have obviously heard about our 2B emergency and are going to be here in about...' she checked her watch '...ten minutes to coddle me for the night.'

'That's nice of them,' Callum murmured.

Hailey nodded. Yes, it was. But she'd been coddled to death when she'd first arrived back from the UK and she was over it a little. It's why she'd struck out on her own. To show them she was fine. 'This place is a mess, though,' she groaned, looking around quickly and shifting her leg to get up.

Callum kept his hand firmly on her shin. He gave her apartment a quick visual once-over. It wasn't too bad. 'Looks OK to me.'

'The kitchen has two days' worth of dirty dishes piled on the sink and I haven't vacuumed in for ever,' she protested.

'Would your sisters care about that?'

'Well, no. But it is Rilla's place and she's a bit of a neat freak, and I'd hate her to think I wasn't looking after it.'

Callum shook his head. He remembered the complete and utter wasteland he'd lived in for those first six months after Annie had died when he'd barely been able to put one foot in front of the other and had been desperately tired from a baby who had just never seemed to sleep. He was relatively immune to mess.

'Well, I don't think either of them would want you hobbling around on a freshly sprained ankle, making the place pretty for them.' The doorbell rang and he saw Hailey start. 'And it appears they're early. Too late now.'

'Great,' Hailey grumbled, moving to push herself up again.

Callum restrained her gently, his hand pushing firmly against her leg. He stood. 'I'll get the door.'

Hailey opened her mouth to protest. Her sisters would get totally the wrong idea. But Callum was almost at the door so she shut her eyes and wished herself anywhere but there.

Callum opened the door to two women and a baby. The shorter one, who looked quite similar to Hailey, was laden with three mouth-wateringly aromatic pizza boxes. 'Hi,' he said to their startled faces.

'Er, hi.' Rilla frowned, looking around the man in her sister's doorway trying to locate Hailey. Her gaze came back to rest on the stranger. She clicked her fingers. 'Tuxedo man.'

It was Callum's turn to frown. 'Callum,' he said, holding out his hand. 'Callum Craig.'

'You're Callum Craig?' Rilla asked, shaking the proffered hand.

Beth turned to her sister for clarification. 'The one who helped her today? The paediatrician?'

Rilla nodded. 'Apparently.'

They turned to look at him and he felt like he was a specimen placed under a microscope. He shook the other sister's hand, mindful not to wake the sleeping baby as they introduced themselves. 'Hailey had a little accident on the stairs. I was just getting her settled.'

Rilla and Beth didn't wait for him to step aside, brushing past him in a hurry at his news.

'Hailey!' Beth called.

'It's OK,' Hailey said from the lounge, having been privy to the excruciatingly embarrassing doorway introductions. 'I'm fine. It's just a mild sprain.'

There was much bluster and fussing for five minutes as Callum and Hailey filled them in on what had happened. Bridie woke up with all the noise and Beth sat on the lounge opposite her sister to feed the baby. Tom was utterly fascinated and sat next to Beth with rapt attention, gently stroking Bridie's forehead as she nursed.

'Anyway, we should be going,' Callum said when he could get a word in edgeways. 'Come on, Tom.'

'Oh, no, Daddy, please, not yet,' he begged.

Beth smiled at the earnest expression on Tom's face. 'Stay,' she urged. 'Let us feed you. It's the least we can do for the assistance you rendered our sister. We have plenty. We always buy more—Hailey's favourite food is cold pizza,' she teased.

'It is not,' Hailey protested, blushing. Although it was up there.

'Please, Daddy.'

Callum could feel himself weakening. It had been a long time since he'd been enveloped in such family hospitality. And he still found it hard to say no to Tom. He glanced at Hailey.

Hailey wanted Beth to take back the invitation. She didn't want to dine with him. She didn't want him to be privy to the intimacy of her family. She wanted him to leave. But her sisters were right. He had been terrifically helpful and it seemed churlish to kick him out when they had enough food to feed an army. 'Join us,' she said, forcing a welcoming smile to her lips. 'Please.'

Callum fought temptation for a few seconds and then succumbed. 'Sure. Thanks. Tom loves pizza too.'

Tom cheered and startled Bridie, who protested the loss of her food supply before she found the nipple again.

'How can I help?' Callum asked Rilla.

'You can grab some plates,' she replied.

Hailey watched in dismay as Callum and Rilla disappeared into the kitchen, the feeling that things were spinning out of her control taking a firm hold. 'So, Callum, you do house calls?' she heard Rilla ask, and she groaned out loud.

Hailey didn't taste a single morsel of the delicious gourmet pizza that was served. The conversation eddied and flowed around her and she felt as if she was in the middle of a whirlpool, sucked along, buffeted by the ripples everyone else was making with no control over their direction.

She nodded in the right places, murmured words that seemed to be required of her but inside her head her brain was spinning, sloshing from one side to the other, always a few seconds behind. She felt a slight headache take up residence and she massaged her forehead to relieve the building pressure.

'Are you OK?' Callum murmured, noticing the movement.

Hailey started a little at his deep voice so close to her ear and wished again that he'd decided to sit on the other side of the lounge. With her taking up one sofa and Rilla and Beth taking up the other, Callum had opted for the floor. He was currently propped up against the arm of her chair, his long legs stretched out in front, crossed at the ankles.

'I'm fine,' she dismissed quickly.

Callum didn't think she looked fine at all but took that as his cue to rejoin the conversation. He glanced over at Tom, lying in front of the television, and then returned his attention to the women. It was fascinating stuff, trying to work out the dynamics of Hailey's family. The sisters' interactions were interesting, their verbal and non-verbal communication telling of a very close relationship.

Beth and Rilla teased Hailey mercilessly. They joked about her shopping addiction, her fondness for eighties disco music, her party-girl existence and her string of short-lived boyfriends. Hailey seemed distracted, responding automatically, but neither sister seemed to notice, the routine obviously familiar to them all.

Callum was surprised. The fun-loving Hailey that Beth and Rilla obviously knew and loved was not the Hailey he had seen. He remembered the New Year's Eve party. She'd been serious—solemn even. And she'd most certainly been alone. The picture her sisters painted just didn't fit in with the first impressions he had already formed.

What had happened to her?

His musings were interrupted by a cry of distress from Tom. He looked up to find his son wild-eyed in front of him, tears trekking down his cheeks.

'My orchie, Daddy. I've lost orchie.'

Callum felt his gut clench at the distress in his son's voice. He pulled him down onto his lap and cuddled him close. 'It's OK, Tommy, it was just here—it can't be too far away.'

Hailey saw the look in Tom's eyes and was surprised to see something akin to panic. She'd wondered about the connection to the rather austere object. Was it some kind of comfort toy? Like a favourite teddy or a soft blanket? She glanced at Rilla and Beth, who looked equally bewildered.

She'd been aware of a hard object pressing into her good foot for a while and suddenly it clicked as to what it was. Tom's torch. He must have dropped it there when he'd been shining it on her injury earlier.

She bent at the waist to retrieve it. 'Ahh! Look what I've found!' Hailey exclaimed.

'Orchie! Orchie!' Tom beamed, grabbing it from Hailey and hugging it close.

'Tom,' Callum chided gently. 'It's not polite to snatch. Say thank you to Hailey.'

'Oh, thank you, Hailey. Thank you!' Tom said, and flung his arms around her neck.

The torch was squashed into her chest and Hailey wondered if there would be a bruise there in the morning, but Tom's high little voice, full of gratitude, overrode any discomfort. His little skinny arms trembled as they clung to her and Hailey held him tight.

'OK, Tom.' Callum laughed, pulling him off Hailey's neck. 'You've got orchie, now go back and watch the telly.'

Tom nodded and skipped away happily. No one would

have ever guessed that a minute ago he'd looked on the verge of a nervous breakdown.

'I'm sorry,' Callum apologised to Hailey. 'He's very attached to it.'

Hailey rubbed absently at the spot just below her shoulder where the imprint of the torch was still making itself felt. 'Like a security blanket?' she murmured.

Callum nodded. He looked up, seeing the curious looks over Tom's attachment to something as non-cuddly as a torch. He glanced over at his son again to check that he was too absorbed in the show to be listening.

'Tom was diagnosed with ALL two years ago. He had a lot of complications and spent quite a bit of time in hospital. At night, on the ward, it was dark and he'd wake up really frightened. One of the nurses suggested I buy him a torch, give him back some control. I'm afraid they still can't be parted.'

Hailey felt as if the walls were closing in. Acute lympho-cytic leukaemia? She heard the gasps and the sympathetic murmurs from her sisters but was too frozen to respond. *Tom was sick?*

'Is his treatment complete?' Rilla asked.

'Six months now,' Callum confirmed. He didn't say what the three nurses would have already known. Tom needed five years in remission to be given the all-clear. He could relapse at any moment.

Hailey stared at him unblinkingly. Tom was sick? It felt like déjà vu. She remembered Eric. How his meningitis had developed out of the blue and he'd been dead within two days. How the love she'd once felt for Paul, Eric's father, had been mangled by the vortex of grief, guilt and blame.

Hailey vaguely heard Callum mentioning his wife's

battle with cancer but was still too stunned over the information on Tom to really compute this latest tidbit. Callum
had certainly been through a harrowing six years. If it had
been anything like this last year for her, she was amazed
he was still standing.

Oh, dear God. She was doing it again. Becoming attracted to a man with a sick child. A sick, motherless child.
Becoming? Who was she kidding? There was no becoming
about it. She was. She'd arrived. She was attracted to him.
But this was worse than with Paul. Much worse. She'd
known Callum for a week and she could barely think about
anything else.

For heaven's sake, he'd sat beside her all evening and
she couldn't recall a thing anyone had said. This was no
friendship evolving into something else, no slow burn, as
it had been with Paul. This was a raging bush fire set to
explode out of control. Last time had crushed her and
already she knew this wasn't in the same league. She
couldn't survive another doomed attraction.

'Isn't that right, Hailey?'

'Wh-what?' Hailey spun around, Beth's voice intruding
into her seething thoughts.

'I was saying how you saw Remi Duconte speak in
London about the advances in leukaemia treatments.'

'Er…yes.' Hailey nodded, trying to think of a single
thing the world's foremost expert in childhood cancer had
had to say.

Callum glanced at Hailey. She seemed nervous suddenly. Out of it. Her replies were automatic, like those
of a robot. Had the news of Tom's illness thrown her that
badly?

'He's in Brisbane soon, isn't he? Dad's chairing his

lecture,' Beth added, oblivious to the conflict raging inside her younger sister.

'Tomorrow night.' Hailey nodded absently.

'I assume you're going?' Beth asked Callum.

Callum shook his head. 'I'm registered to attend but Tom's grandparents, who normally look after him, have tickets to *Les Misérables* tomorrow night. I'll catch him next time.'

'Oh, but you simply must go!' Beth urged. 'Aside from your work, you have such a personal stake in it.'

'Yes. I will be disappointed to miss out. He rarely lectures these days. But as I haven't been in Brisbane very long I don't have alternative child-care arrangements yet. I'm afraid the timing's all wrong.'

'Nonsense,' Beth dismissed. 'You know us, don't you?'

Callum laughed. 'Oh, no, really, it's OK. I couldn't impose.'

'Hailey can do it,' Rilla piped up, ignoring Hailey's knitted brows. 'She's just down the hall. She won't mind. She loves kids. Don't you, Hails?'

Callum looked at Hailey. He didn't profess to be an expert on women's moods—and he'd been married for five years—but Hailey looked as if she minded. A lot. She was frowning her disapproval at her sister.

Callum didn't want to rock the family boat and certainly not with Hailey who he felt on rocky ground with anyway. 'No. It's fine, really.'

'Hailey?' Rilla prompted. 'It would be such a shame for Callum to miss it, don't you think?'

Hailey looked at her sister. Just what was Rilla playing at? Wasn't she the one who had warned her against getting involved with another motherless little boy?

But Rilla was right. Seeing Remi Duconte was not an event to be missed and Callum had been as solid as a rock during the emergency today and had then gone on to scrape her up off the floor, help her into her apartment and administer first aid. She sighed. 'Will half six be OK?'

Callum shook his head again. 'No. I couldn't impose.'

'Look, I'm offering,' she said testily. 'This really is one lecture you don't want to miss. Unless you're worried Tom would fret?' Hailey frowned. 'I suppose we've only just met.'

'Oh, no. Since his protracted stint in hospital, Tom isn't particularly bothered about new faces. And he seems to have taken a real shine to you. Besides, you found orchie and let him have two servings of ice cream. You'd better watch out, he'll be moving in next.'

Hailey forced a smile to her lips as her sisters laughed at Callum's joke. 'Excellent. That's settled, then,' she murmured.

Except it wasn't, of course. Was she insane? Things were about as unsettled as the ocean in the middle of a tropical cyclone.

CHAPTER FOUR

HAILEY'S fingers were shaking as she limped to Callum's door and pushed the doorbell promptly at six-thirty the next evening, mentally cursing Rilla. Apparently her middle sister had changed her mind about Hailey's involvement with another man and child. 'Maybe he's just what you need,' Rilla had said last night after Callum had left.

She gave herself a shake. *It's just two hours. That's all. One hundred and twenty minutes. You can do this.*

The door flung open and Tom stood there in his pyjamas, his damp hair plastered to his forehead, trusty torch in hand.

'Hailey!' Tom threw his six-year-old body at her, hugging her around the waist, crushing his torch against her hip bone.

'Tom,' she said, looking down at his sandy-blond head, wincing at the bite of the hard plastic.

His little arms felt good around her waist and though they were skinny his grip was strong. Despite his pallor, Tom seemed so vital. Her heart squeezed painfully in her chest at the thought of him ill and frightened, clutching his torch late at night on some big scary oncology ward.

Callum had said Tom had spent a lot of time in hospital

so it sounded as if he'd had a stormy course during his treatments. Had he been plagued with debilitating nausea? Or fallen prey to any of the side effects of chemotherapy? Had he lost his hair?

She ruffled his damp locks. Damn it. She didn't want to know any of this. She wasn't supposed to be getting involved any more.

'OK, Tom.' Callum laughed, amused at his son's delight. 'You were supposed to be cleaning your teeth.'

Hailey looked up to find him lounging against a nearby doorframe. The man was looking good enough to eat. He was wearing jeans and an untucked short-sleeved shirt with stripes. His arms looked bulky and very, very touchable. His very short hair emphasised the chiselled planes of his face. She could smell soap and aftershave.

His feet were bare, adding to his casual appeal. Damn it! How could feet be so alluring, for crying out loud? He blasted her with a slow, sexy smile and she almost turned and ran. In fact, had her ankle been up to it, she might have seriously considered it.

She swallowed. 'Hi.'

Callum inclined his head. She looked tense, hanging onto the doorknob like it was a lifeline. She was wearing a floral skirt that flared around her knees and a navy T-shirt that clung to the generous swell of her breasts. He felt a pull in his groin at her fresh-faced, damp-haired appeal and a punch to his gut at the way Tom clung to her like he'd known her all his life. 'Hi.'

They stared at each other for a few moments. 'Teeth,' Callum ordered Tom breaking eye contact with Hailey.

Tom skipped away and they watched him until he disappeared from sight. Callum returned his attention to Hailey. She gave him a tight smile.

'How's your ankle?' he asked politely.

'It's much better, thank you. The swelling's gone down considerably and I can put most of my weight on it,' she replied just as politely.

Callum almost laughed. Their stilted conversation would have done two strangers proud. Except they weren't. Yesterday they'd saved a life and a few days before that he had kissed her. 'You know, I can cancel going to this thing.'

'No.' Hailey shook her head automatically. 'It's fine.'

Callum sighed. 'It's patently obvious you don't want to be here, Hailey.'

'No, really, I…' What? I what? I'm looking forward to it? *I want nothing more than to babysit your not-out-of-the-woods-yet adorable six-year-old?*

'Hailey, I'm hardly likely to leave my son with a woman who looks like she'd rather have a hole drilled in her head.'

She felt a shaft of guilt lance her chest. She closed her eyes briefly and shut the door. 'I'm sorry. Go. Really. I'm not… I mean…' Hailey looked at him looking at her expectantly. Waiting for her to say something that would make her behaviour less odd. Unfortunately, she couldn't think of a damn thing. 'You wouldn't understand.'

Callum put his hands on his hips. 'Try me.'

'Tooth's done, Daddy.'

Tom's chirpy interruption was just what Hailey needed to pull herself together. She'd almost said something really stupid. Like, *I feel insanely attracted to you and I'm petrified.*

Callum shut his eyes briefly, inwardly cursing Tom's bad timing. He crouched down. 'Open up,' he said.

Tom opened his mouth and Callum inspected his son's job. 'Looks good, Tommy.' He pulled him close for a hug and inhaled the sweet smell of bubblebath and baby powder. His heart ached in his chest as Tom wrapped his arms around his neck and held on tight.

They were a team. He and Tom. They'd been alone for most of Tom's young life and been through some very tough times. Tom desperately wanted a mother—and a baby brother—but Callum just wasn't in the market for a relationship, no matter how much Hailey had revived his libido.

Losing Annie had been hard and he didn't want to set himself up for any more heartache. He certainly wouldn't be stupid enough to fall for someone who had 'Keep out' written all over her. He didn't need someone in his life who had even more baggage than him.

'C'mon, Hailey.' Tom squirmed out of his father's embrace and took his reluctant babysitter's hand. 'Do you like reading? Can you read to me?'

Hailey's gaze locked with Callum's for a brief moment before she dragged it away. 'I like reading best of all.' Hailey pulled her own book out of her bag and waggled it, grinning down at Tom.

'I like it the mostest too,' Tom agreed, tugging on Hailey's hand, dragging her hobbling form into the lounge.

Callum left them to it, gathering his stuff, slipping on some shoes. He wandered into the kitchen and placed Tom's plate and cutlery into the dishwasher. Tom's laughter drifted in to him and he lounged in the archway between the two rooms for a few minutes.

Although they had their backs to him, he could easily see them snuggled in a single armchair, Tom firmly ensconced on Hailey's lap, their heads close together. They were reading Tom's favourite book about animal mothers. Hailey laughed at something Tom said and Tom pointed at a picture.

She was a natural with him. So why hadn't she been comfortable with the idea of babysitting him? Why the reticence when she'd first arrived? Was it Tom or was it to do with him? With them. With the insane attraction that was between them?

'How come you're not a mummy, Hailey? Beth has Birdie and Rilla's going to be a mummy soon.'

Callum closed his eyes. Six-year-olds weren't exactly known for their tact. He opened his mouth to tell Tom to mind his own business but shut it instead, curious to know the answer.

Hailey's hand stilled on the page. Just like a kid to cut to the chase. 'I almost was,' she said, her pulse reverberating loudly through her head. 'A few years back. But then it didn't happen.'

Callum straightened. Almost? Had Hailey had a miscarriage? Was this the sorrow he sensed she carried with her? Was this why looking after Tom was so hard?

'My mummy's dead.'

Callum shut his eyes. It was so matter-of-fact. So childlike. Spoken with no emotion from a little boy who had no true concept of what a mother was. *It was so unfair.*

Hailey nodded slowly. 'Yes, I know. That's very sad.'

'It would have been good having a mummy in hospital. I was scared.'

Callum sucked in a breath. Tom had never verbalised that before.

Hailey noted Tom's vice-like grip on his torch and her heart went out to him. 'You're lucky you have a very special daddy who was there for you.'

Tom nodded. 'A mummy would have been good too. For Daddy also. He misses her. Grandma says so and he goes all googoo-eyed sometimes when he thinks I'm not watching.'

Hailey smiled at the description despite the heaviness in her heart. Another man still in love with his wife—she sure knew how to pick 'em.

Callum pushed off the wall. OK—that was definitely enough! 'Right, well, I'm off,' he said, forcing a cheery note into his voice as he advanced into the room from behind them.

Hailey blushed. She felt like she'd been caught prying, fishing for background info. She hadn't asked for any of it and she most certainly didn't want to know it. All it did was give this little boy and his father an even bigger inroad to her heart, and that was the last thing she wanted.

'Are you sure?' Callum asked Hailey again. He hoped he looked normal. Not like he'd been eavesdropping.

Hailey looked at him, feeling nervous and all fluttery inside. Poor Callum had been through the mill and Tom's innocent admission that Callum still missed his wife made her heart ache for him. 'It'll be fine,' she said quietly over Tom's head. 'Just go.'

Callum nodded. He crossed to say goodnight to his son. 'You be good for Hailey, OK?' Callum leaned down to drop a kiss on Tom's head. Hailey's cleavage came into view and her scent, like raindrops on roses, enveloped him. He pulled away sharply after the merest of pecks.

'Yes, Daddy.'

'Another half hour,' Callum said, clearing his throat, not daring to look at Hailey. 'Then bed.'

'Oh, but, Daddy…'

Callum laughed and tousled his son's hair. 'No, "oh-but-daddys".'

'Thanks,' he said, forcing himself to look Hailey in the eye. 'Have you eaten?'

'I'm not really hungry,' she said, still recovering from the brief moment when his face had been, oh, so close to hers.

'Well, if you do develop an appetite, feel free to help yourself to anything you want in the kitchen.'

Hailey nodded, absently brushing her chin against the crown of Tom's head. His hair was soft and smelled like soap.

'I've left my mobile number on the fridge. In case.'

Hailey stilled as Callum said goodbye to Tom and headed for the door. In case? In case of what? She felt a nudge of worry spike her bloodstream and kick her pulse up a notch. Tom hadn't been well. He'd had leukaemia with a complicated course of treatment. What if he got sick while she was looking after him? Like Eric had?

She quickly moved Tom and settled him in the armchair, then hurried to catch Callum at the front door. 'You mean in case he gets sick?' she said, her voice low.

Callum smiled. 'Or falls out of a tree. Or breaks his arm. Or cuts a major artery. You know, the usual.'

Except he wasn't likely to do anything of those things, was he? Tom was hardly usual. But he could relapse at any stage. 'What if he gets a fever or becomes lethargic?'

Oh, God, how did he do it? How did he let go after Tom had been so sick? How did he ever leave him? Why wasn't he constantly worried, constantly alarmed at the things that could befall a kid whose immune system had been completely wiped out not that long ago? 'What if…what if he gets a rash?'

Callum's smile died on his lips when he met her unblinking gaze. Hailey's alarm was genuine. Why should any of those things concern an experienced paediatric nurse? Annie's mother maybe, but Hailey? He frowned. Was that what was freaking her out? Why she had been reluctant to come tonight? To get involved with them? Tom's illness? Had losing her baby made her hyper-vigilant?

'I'm only going to be gone for two hours, Hailey,' he said gently. 'I'm sure no calamity will strike in that time that you can't handle.'

Hailey felt the cold hand of fear clutch at her gut. What if she couldn't? What if she missed something? An image of Eric lying critically ill on a ventilator played on her inward eye. Paul's gut-wrenching grief echoed in her head.

'Hailey.'

Callum's strong, confident voice reached through her escalating panic. She looked at him.

'Tom's in remission. He's fine. Look at him. Nothing's going to happen to him while I'm out.'

Hailey held Callum's gaze for a few moments before forcing herself to look down at Tom. Tom, who had come to find her, book in hand. He chose that moment to look up at her and smile one of his cheeky smiles. Callum was right. He did look fine.

But her confidence had taken a real hit when Eric had fallen ill so quickly. It had taken many months to trust her instincts again. To realise that no one could have foreseen the rapid onset of the meningitis that had claimed his young life.

She took some deep, calming breaths. 'Of course.' She shot him a confident smile. The second last thing he needed other than thinking she'd rather have a hole drilled in her head was that he was leaving his son with a complete basket case. 'Of course. Go. We'll be fine, won't we, Tommy?'

Tom nodded and they went back to the armchair. Callum lingered. He could see Hailey had relaxed. She had begun reading to Tom again, putting on a funny voice as she read the words.

Hailey read on aware of his scrutiny. 'You'll miss it,' she said as Tom turned the page. She didn't bother to look up.

Callum took her cue and left but the uneasy feeling persisted. The trouble was it didn't have much to do with Hailey's moment of doubt and everything to do with how good it felt to see them snuggled on the chair together, their heads close, laughing like they'd been doing it for years.

After her initial insecurities Hailey took to babysitting Tom with all the ease of someone very used to minding children. She allowed him to push the boundaries of his bedtime and they read for nearly an hour after Callum left.

When it came to calling a halt, Tom, obviously struggling to stay awake, didn't protest. She pulled back his bedcovers, shut his window and tucked him in. He looked very cute, snuggled into the bedclothes, his torch held securely in one hand.

'Can you lay with me till I go to sleep, Hailey?' Tom asked drowsily.

Her heart squeezed in her chest. How could she resist such a request when Tom was looking at her with his big blue eyes? Eyes that had seen too much in his short little life.

'Move over, then.' She smiled hoping she wasn't breaking any house rules. She had often lain with Eric as he had drifted off to sleep and a small part of her heart desperately wanted to feel a little body snuggled into her again.

Tom wriggled over and Hailey curled her body around

his, one arm around his waist, her other elbow bent, her head propped up on her hand. Hailey watched him fall sleep.

She'd always been nuts about kids, hence her interest in midwifery then paediatrics. The fact that she was now an aunt and due to become so again in the very near future had been a major cause for excitement in her life.

Not that long ago she'd even looked forward to having her own tribe to dote on. But the incident with Eric had made her realise that the loss of a child was utterly devastating. And she never wanted to leave herself open to that kind of hurt again. Ever.

She yawned. Sleep had been elusive since the ball. Last night's slumber had been worst of all because of her ankle and Callum's revelations. Her eyelids felt heavy. Surely it wouldn't matter if she shut her eyes for a moment? She dropped her head onto the pillow, nuzzling the back of Tom's head, his locks tickling her nose. She burrowed in closer to his little body, sighing contently as she fell deeply asleep.

Callum arrived home to a darkened house at nearly nine o'clock. He carried a bag of Chinese take-aways. He wasn't sure if Hailey had eaten already or even if she was allergic to MSG, but the least he could do was feed her for helping him out of a tight spot.

'I'm home,' he called as he shut the door. There wasn't an answer and Hailey wasn't in the lounge room. He frowned, feeling a needle of unease prick at him. He dumped the bags of food in the kitchen and wandered towards his son's room, urging himself to stay calm.

He pulled up short when he discovered a sleeping Hailey curled up in Tom's bed, her arm around his son's waist. He felt his heart flop in his chest and his breath stutter to a halt.

They looked like they belonged together. A stranger could be forgiven for pegging them as mother and son.

His chest hurt and he realised he hadn't taken a breath. He ordered himself to do so and allowed fresh air to fill his lungs. It felt weird to be looking down at something that should be a natural sight. Tom, curled up with his mother. But apart from those precious first few months of Tom's life, Callum had no memories like this. And Hailey wasn't his mother.

Callum turned on his heel, hightailing it out of Tom's room, his mind spinning. He unpacked the take-aways, trying to wrap his head around the twists of his life. He'd been so certain the move from Melbourne had been exactly what they'd both needed. A change of pace. Putting the past and all its tragedies behind and forging a new future in a new town together. The job at the Brisbane General had been perfect. And Annie had always wanted to move to sunnier climes.

He'd known too that her parents had always hankered to retire in Queensland. But he'd also known they'd never move so far away from Tom. So far away from their one tangible connection to their daughter. So the decision, in the end, had been an easy one.

But he hadn't expected this. A girl called Hailey coming into his life, kissing him on a balcony and cuddling Tom, getting under his skin, making him want things he hadn't thought about in for ever. Tonight she looked as if she belonged here in his apartment.

He missed being part of a couple. He hadn't realised it until now. All those intimacies of living together. The gentle touches, the secret smiles, the knowing looks, the innate synchronicity that happened when one person knew the other so completely. He hadn't hadn't had time to think about it since Annie had died. He certainly hadn't had time to want it. But looking at Hailey asleep with Tom, it was all he could think about.

Maybe this had been Annie's grand plan for him? He used to talk to her. A lot. In the beginning. But then Tom had fallen ill and existing had been all he could manage. Annie and his grief had faded even further as everything to do with Tom had taken over.

He gave himself a mental shake and left the kitchen, sitting himself down in the chair where Hailey and Tom had been earlier. He sat forward, his elbows bent on his knees, his face cradled in his palms. This was insane. He barely knew her. And he certainly didn't know how to date and do the daddy thing.

All presuming that she'd want to. Which, given her reticence to babysit, didn't seem likely. Hailey had significant baggage, he'd heard as much tonight. And Tom and he had enough of their own. Above all else he had to think of Tom first. And as much as Tom adored Hailey, it didn't mean it was reciprocated.

His gaze fell on the book that Hailey had brought with her to read. It was a memoir and he flipped through it absently while his thoughts chased each other into a giant jumble. A slip of paper fell out from between two of the pages and he picked it up off the floor.

He frowned. It wasn't paper. It was a photograph. Hailey was cuddling a little boy who was laughing up at her. The boy looked about Tom's age and the spitting image of the man who was also laughing, his arm draped possessively around her shoulder.

Callum's heartbeat pounded through his veins, his curiosity piqued. He knew this was none of his business but the image was captivating. Who were those people in the photo with Hailey? Was the man a lover? Her husband? Had she been married? Was the little boy hers? What had happened to him? Was she grieving too? Was this what she'd alluded to with Tom earlier? What had Hailey been through?

So many questions. So many reasons to run a mile. And yet he still felt drawn to her. Why? He replaced the photo in the book and wandered back into Tom's room, looking for answers. He stood at the end of the bed, observing a sleeping Hailey.

Man! She was seriously gorgeous. In sleep all her defences had been stripped away. The frown he saw on her face a little too frequently was gone, her delectable mouth, too often pulled tight, was slack and inviting. He had a feeling he was seeing the real Hailey.

But who was the real Hailey? The efficient nurse? The younger sister? The reluctant babysitter? The laughing woman in the photo with the mystery man and child? And what the hell did it matter? He didn't need a woman in his life. He'd already had one, found happiness with one. It was greedy to expect more, surely?

He glanced at his sleeping son, grateful to still have him. Losing his wife had been heart-breaking. To have lost Tom too…that would have been soul-destroying. He usually daren't wish for anything more. Except right now, with Hailey asleep in Tom's bed, he wished he had a crystal ball or a magic wand. He wished he could go back and make everything right. For both of them.

Hailey murmured as if his wish had disturbed her as it had passed by. He mentally tossed up whether to wake her or not. His heart told him to let her sleep. But his gut doubted whether she'd appreciate the gesture. Yes, she got on with Tom. If he had to bet the apartment on it, he'd even say she liked him. But he'd be blind and stupid to not realise she was there only through sibling pressure.

He wondered for a moment, though, what it would be like to be allowed the liberty of kissing her awake. To feel her mouth curve into a smile beneath his, her arms creep up around his neck.

He shut his eyes against the vision and gripped the end of the bed. 'Hailey?' he called.

She didn't stir so he moved closer, crouching beside the bed and giving her shoulder a shake. Hailey stirred again, muttering to herself, turning in the bed so she now faced him, his eyes level with her cleavage. He shut them and prayed for restraint. When he opened them he noticed how the T-shirt pulled across her chest, causing the three little buttons to gape and show a glimpse of purple satin. 'Hailey,' he said again.

It took a few seconds for Callum's voice to penetrate the fog of sleep clinging to her. But then she was instantly awake. She sat up as if she'd been hit by an electric cattle prod.

'Whoa!' Callum chuckled, startled by her sudden motion and her wide-eyed demeanour. 'Shh. Don't wake Tom. I'm sorry, I didn't mean to frighten you.'

Hailey felt disorientation fuddle her senses for a moment before clarity hit her. She'd fallen asleep in Tom's bed? What must Callum think? It was too…too intimate. 'Oh, God. I'm so sorry,' she gasped, trying to ignore her gut reaction to Callum in the darkened room.

'It's OK.' He smiled and moved so she could get off the bed. 'I do it all the time. You must have been tired.'

'Mmm.' She yawned her head still foggy. She stood in

the doorway and watched while Callum pulled the sheets up over Tom and stroked his cheek. It was such a simple gesture but the love behind it clawed at her heart.

He came and stood in the doorway with her and they both watched Tom sleep for a few more moments.

'Oh, man, what smells so good?' Hailey asked, turning to look up at Callum. He smiled at her and in the half-light his mouth looked plain wicked.

'Chinese. I bought enough for two. I thought you might not have eaten yet. Come on, I'll serve up.'

Hailey blinked at his retreating back. Well, she hadn't eaten and she was starving, but she must have been more disorientated than she'd thought to be even considering sharing a meal with a man whose lips looked like pure sin in the subdued lighting.

She heard the clinking dishes and the spicy aroma of Chinese food wafted towards her.

'Hailey?'

Her stomach growled. She shut her eyes and went to join him in the kitchen.

CHAPTER FIVE

CALLUM PUSHED a plate at her. 'Here you go. What do you want to drink?'

'Oh,' she said, taking the proffered plate, knowing it would be churlish to refuse when he'd already dished up. 'Water's fine, thank you.'

He poured her a tall glass and cracked the lid on a long-necked beer for himself. 'Let's eat in the lounge. Ladies first.' He gestured.

They made small talk while they ate. She sat in the middle of the three-seater sofa and he sat in the chair where she had read to Tom.

'So how was the lecture?' she asked when a gap in the conversation had gone beyond companionable and watching him eat was sensual torture.

Callum swallowed and hesitated for a moment, trying to sound professional. 'Clinically? Fascinating.'

Hailey looked at him sharply. By the tone of his voice it seemed there was a lot missing in that statement.

'Sounds like there's a "but" there,' she prodded, putting her almost clean plate on the coffee-table that separated them.

Callum sighed, putting his plate down too. 'No. Not really. As a doctor, Remi's lecture was full of information about the latest studies and advances in chemo and promising new treatments. The use of stem cells has so much potential. Remi called them the new frontier.'

Hailey could still hear the distinct lack of enthusiasm in his voice. 'But?'

'From a personal viewpoint, it was as depressing as hell.'

'Oh.' Hailey hadn't thought of that. As a father who had watched his child endure the rigours of chemotherapy, it must have been a hard subject to warm to.

'I mean, I wanted to go, to be informed. More for Tom than for any professional reasons. But it just reminded me, despite all the advances and the successes, what a horrible illness leukaemia is. And what his chances are if he relapses. It bought back…memories.'

Hailey swallowed. Callum was staring into the distance, his grey gaze stormy. 'It was bad?'

Callum turned and looked at her directly. 'It felt like my heart was being ripped out.' *Again.*

'I'm sorry.'

Callum went back to staring at the far wall. 'He developed a lot of complications, picked up every infection going and ended up in ICU for a while.'

He stopped and looked up at her. 'He looked so small and still. He didn't even look like Tom. His hair fell out and he lost weight and he just looked like this haggard bag of bones.'

Hailey, her fingers trailing restlessly along the frosty sides of her glass, stayed silent even though she didn't want to. She wanted to stop him. To tell him she didn't want to know any of this stuff. She had enough fodder for her nightmares without adding mental pictures of a bald, skeletal Tom.

Callum noted her shuttered gaze and gave a sharp half-laugh, his lips twisting as he rolled his cold bottle of beer against his forehead. 'I'm sorry. You don't want to hear this.'

Hailey shrugged, resigned to her fate. Compelled to listen almost as strongly as she was repulsed. 'No. It's OK. It sounds like you need to talk. I think sometimes it's easier to talk to a stranger.'

What would she give to be able to unburden some of her deepest, darkest thoughts when the weight of them got too much to bear?

'But you're not a stranger, are you?'

His midnight kiss whispered its treachery into her ear. 'As good as.'

Callum didn't think for a moment that she believed that. He was pretty certain she was as aware of the tension between them as him. But she had a valid point. Why was he unburdening himself to her? He hadn't spoken to anyone about the emotional roller-coaster of the last couple of years.

People had been so concerned that he was going to fall apart after the death of Annie that he'd been working double time to prove to everyone that he was OK. Even when the leukaemia whammy had been served up to him he'd soldiered on, pretending he was fine. Being strong for Tom. For Annie's parents.

They'd been devastated. They were elderly and he knew that life had thrown them one too many curve balls when Tom had become ill. He'd made sure he'd kept himself together for them especially. Between them and Tom and well-meaning friends, he hadn't had any time to dwell on the unfairness of the hand life had dealt him.

Maybe it was because Hailey wasn't going to fall all

over him and shower him with pity. Maybe her reluctance to get involved with him and Tom made her a perfect sounding board. Maybe she was right, and the stranger factor removed any need to mentally edit his words. Or maybe he was just over burying it inside and she was in the wrong place at the wrong time.

'I used to watch him during the night. Watching his little chest rise and fall. Rise and fall. He's such a shallow breather. I was terrified he'd just stop.'

'You couldn't have got much sleep.'

Callum laughed and took a pull of his beer. 'No. I don't think I've slept a full night in six years.'

'You didn't sleep well after…after your wife… I'm sorry, I don't know her name.'

'Annie.'

'After Annie died?'

Callum looked at her. 'You know, you're about the only person who's spoken her name to me in years. They usually just fade off or say er and um a lot while they look at their feet.'

Hailey gave a ghost of a smile. 'I suppose people don't want to upset you.'

'I suppose.'

They were silent for a few moments. 'What was she like? Your Annie?'

He looked down at his hands. He hadn't spoken about her in such a long time to anyone. 'Incredible. Vital. Funny. Strong. She fought. She fought hard. Even right at the end she was positive. Cracking jokes and telling everyone it was going to be OK. Trying to make it easier for me and Tom.'

He was silent for a while and Hailey felt humbled by

the ghost of Annie. *She* hadn't fought. She'd run away. She hadn't been strong. She'd been weak. Maybe she should have fought harder? 'How did you meet?'

'At uni.' He smiled, remembering. 'She was a philosophy major. She thought all med students were egomaniacs.'

Hailey laughed. 'She was wise, too.'

Callum smiled as memories tripped through his head. 'She certainly put me through my paces.'

'She sounds amazing.'

'Yeah. She was. I just wish…'

Hailey didn't need to hear his wish. He was still in love with his wife, that much was obvious. Just like Paul had still been in love with his.

'By the time we discovered her cancer it was already in her bones and liver. In fact, jaundice was her first symptom. It was so futile. But she was determined to soldier on, to do things for herself, to not let me see how scared she was. Still, there were times when she didn't know I was watching that she would hold Tom and look at him with this expression…knowing…knowing she was dying and she wouldn't be around for him.'

Hailey watched him, his head downcast. She could only imagine how awful it must have been for Annie to know she was never going to see her son grow up. 'It must have been a very invasive carcinoma,' she said quietly.

'It was.'

'Her pregnancy hormones must have had an impact on its growth.'

'Yep. Accelerated it tenfold. She was dead four months after diagnosis.'

'Callum.' She reached out and touched his arm. 'I'm so sorry.'

Callum nodded. There wasn't much else to say. Life sucked sometimes. He knew that better than most.

'So,' Hailey said, rousing them both from their thoughts. 'You haven't slept much since Annie died?'

Callum rubbed his hands over his scalp and laughed at her abrupt change of conversation. 'Tom had reflux. And colic. And was a night owl. I walked a lot of floorboards and bought a lot of useless, unnecessary late-night infomercial rubbish.'

Hailey laughed. Maybe she shouldn't. He was talking about Annie and Tom's illness and being a single father, but just imagining him pacing late at night, Tom in one arm, his credit card in the other, was exceedingly comic.

Callum laughed too. It felt good to laugh in the midst of the memories that even if they'd been happy were now for ever tinged with grief. 'Good sympathetic ear you are,' he mocked.

Hailey tried to model her face into instant contrition and failed. 'I'm sorry.'

Callum chuckled. 'It's OK. Really. People have tiptoed around me for six years. It's nice to be with someone who doesn't say the right thing.'

'Thank you.' She frowned. 'I think.'

He laughed again. 'So what about you, Hailey Winters? What's your story? Do you have anything you wish to unburden?' He glanced at the book sitting on the coffee-table, the photo inside.

Hailey sobered. *Did he have all night?* But her history paled in comparison to his. A dead wife and a son with a potentially fatal disease beat a broken heart and the death of a non-related child.

'Come on, Hailey. I heard you telling Tom tonight you

were nearly a mother and then I was flipping through this book earlier.' He picked it up. 'And this photo fell out.' He located it and passed it to her.

Hailey stared at the picture. She'd forgotten the photo was even there. She'd bought the book while she'd been living in England and had never managed to finish it. She'd brought it home with her when she had fled. She looked at Callum and felt strangely compelled to tell him. He had opened up to her. Maybe it would help to talk about it with someone who knew the meaning of grief.

Callum noted her hesitation, the emotion clouding her soft brown gaze. 'Is that your husband? Your son?'

She shook her head. 'No. Eric was my charge. I was his nanny. He died in my care.'

There. She'd said it. Said what no one else would. Not her parents. Or her sisters. And not Paul. Paul's eyes, his withdrawal from her, had said more than his words ever could. She gave him a direct look. A look that dared him to refute it.

Callum was aware of the slow thud of his heart in his chest. 'Could you back up? I think you missed a few steps.'

Hailey nodded wondering where to start as her thumb brushed lightly back and forth over Eric's dear sweet little face in the photo. They'd all been so happy that day.

'I lived in London for three years. When I left here, I wanted to spread my wings. Try something other than midwifery. I have a counselling degree—'

'Ah. No wonder you're a good listener.' Callum smiled.

Oh, yeah, she was great with other people's problems. 'I worked in a refugee crisis centre for a while, counseling kids. That was really hard work. Not physically, like nursing, more emotionally. You know?'

Callum nodded. He could only begin to imagine the problems kids like that must have.

'Then I got a job at a large London children's hospital in one of their general paeds wards. I did that for just over a year.'

She was silent for a while, like she was trying to order things properly for him. He didn't want to pressure her. He wanted it to come out in her own time, in her own way, like he knew it had to.

'Paul was a pharmacist there. I liked him…a lot. His wife had left him when Eric was a baby and his long-term nanny had left six months before that and Paul hadn't been able to find a good permanent replacement. Eric was five and such a cutie. I'd often go over to their place and hang out with them after work.'

Callum nodded for her to continue, even though he knew where the conversation was going.

'Not long after that Paul asked me if I wanted the nanny job and I jumped at it. I was eager to try something different and though the pay wasn't fantastic it was a live-in position, which meant all my living expenses were taken care of.'

Except there was more to it than that, Callum could tell from the photo. There was an intimacy to the image. A possessiveness in Paul's arm on her shoulder. It spoke of connection, of family.

'You were in love with him?'

Hailey glanced at him, the matter-of-factness in his voice echoed in the neutrality of his facial features. 'We began a relationship a couple of months after I moved in.'

Uhuh! That explained her little speech in the panroom about dating colleagues. It had definitely been a case of once bitten, twice shy.

'Everything was great. Really, really fantastic. Until

about three months before Eric died. His mother turned up on the scene. She wanted to reconcile.'

Hailey would never forget that day as long as she lived. The photo she was holding had been taken the day before Donna's return. They had never been that happy again.

'Oh,' Callum said. What else could he say? It must have been hard for Hailey.

'Paul, he was confused… He wanted to do the right thing by Eric… He ended it with me.' Hailey paused, knowing she had skimmed over the details but the pain and betrayal of that moment still stung nearly two years later. Coming home to find them in bed together. She took a shaky breath. 'They reconciled for a couple of months. I stayed on because of Eric but the situation was getting untenable for me.'

'It must have been hard to have their reconciliation shoved in your face every day,' Callum sympathised.

Hailey nodded. 'It was. But she left again after eight weeks and I'm glad I stayed on. They were both devastated by her desertion. And then less than a month later Eric died.'

Callum regarded Hailey as he took a sip of his beer. She had gone silent, staring hard at the photo in her hand. 'How?' he prompted after a while.

'From meningitis. We'd been out all day, shopping and looking through the Natural History Museum—he really loved that place. He was exhausted. We both were. I didn't think anything of it when he fell asleep in front of the television that afternoon.'

Callum shut his eyes. He could hear the doubt and guilt lacing her voice. It had gone from hesitant but strong to tremulous, husky. He knew the futility of guilt and would have given anything to be able to make her see that it didn't serve any useful purpose.

'And he was still sleeping when his father came home and Paul went to wake him because otherwise he never would have slept that night. He was practically unrouseable.'

She didn't know where they'd come from but tears were running down her cheeks. She wiped at them and looked at the moisture on her fingers. She hadn't cried over this in months.

Callum saw the moisture glisten on her fingertips. No wonder she'd been so antsy about Tom coming down with something while he was out. 'Hailey, the onset of meningitis can be so swift. It can kill in hours.'

She nodded and looked at him. She should have been embarrassed to be showing such raw emotion in front of him but on a primal level she knew that he, of all people, would understand. 'I know that. I do. But it was…so awful. He was on life support for forty-eight hours before he died. And Paul…'

'He blamed you.'

Hailey looked at him sharply. 'He was grieving.'

Callum blinked at her vehement defence. It took a few moments for him to get it. *Ah.* 'You're still in love with him.' He was surprised how much the knowledge affected him.

'No.' Hailey looked away. She shook her head. 'I don't know.'

Callum nodded. It took time. He knew that.

They didn't say anything for a few moments. He watched a few more tears escape and trek unhindered down her face and couldn't bear it any longer. He stood. 'Here.' He held out his hand to her.

Hailey looked up. Way up. Dear God, the man was a giant! 'What?' she asked, her voice husky with emotion.

'I'm going to give you a hug.'

Hailey looked at his outstretched hand as if it was a monster from the deep. She sank further back into the chair.

'Hailey,' Callum said patiently, trying not to be insulted by her obvious aversion to his touch. 'You're crying. I'm offering you an age-old form of comfort. I think a hug is probably OK under the circumstances.'

She looked at his hand again. Heaven only knew, she wanted to take it so badly she could barely see it in front of her. But she wasn't entirely sure a hug could ever be just a hug in such emotionally charged circumstances.

'Doctor's orders.' He grinned, reaching impatiently for her hand lying on the arm of the sofa. He pulled her up and towards him. He couldn't explain it—it just seemed like the right gesture at the right time. It was probably something they both needed.

Except as he enfolded her in his arms he hadn't been prepared for the total and utter cataclysmic impact of her body against his. Yes, he'd been aware of their unspoken attraction but hadn't remotely suspected that a friendly hug could feel so dangerous. Sexy. Sinful. Leaving him wanting more. More than hugging.

Her scent infused his senses. Her diminutive frame worked its way beneath his defences. He could feel her breath and her heartbeat and the imprint of her breasts. He looked down on her dark head pressed to his chest, her hair soft against his shirt. His fingers automatically sought her waist and the curve of her hip felt ripe and lush.

Hailey felt Callum become still as he realised what she'd already known. Their attraction was too strong to withstand something even as simple, as asexual, as a friendly hug. He was everywhere. Filling her up. Her head and her heart and her senses. She clutched his shirt to steady herself as she pressed her face into his chest and inhaled a huge dose of his clean male aroma.

Callum's hands closed convulsively on her hips, sub-consciously drawing her into him. This was insane. 'Hailey,' he croaked, looking down at her.

'Callum we can't—'

He didn't give her a chance to finish, both his hands skimming her face and spearing through her hair as he cut off her protest with the urgent covering of his mouth.

Hailey followed where he led. There was no thought of protest now he had made that first move. Nothing had ever felt this right. His mouth was urgent, desperate, almost frantic on hers, and she matched his pace, moaning deep in her throat as the kiss dripped molten desire into her bloodstream.

She felt him lifting her up, lifting her higher until their heads were level and she felt as if she was kissing him as an equal. On her terms. Giving as well as taking. She bracketed his face in her hands, raking her fingers up into his hair, revelling in the eroticism as his very short spikes grazed the sensitive flesh of her fingertips.

She ran her palm backwards and forwards over his scalp, her hands already addicted to the sensation. He groaned and it emboldened her to push her tongue into his mouth, desperate to taste him, to explore him.

Callum moved, feeling for the lounge, lowering Hailey, placing his knee on the edge and easing her gently back-wards. She clung to him, bringing him down with her, her lips glued to his.

'Hailey,' he gasped, pulling away, a vague sense of pro-priety giving him pause. He leaned his forehead against hers, his breath ragged as her mouth sought his eye, his cheek, his neck. 'This is totally out of control. If you want it to stop, it had better be now.'

She shook her head. It was like a line had been crossed and there was no going back. Hailey sought his mouth. 'No,' she said against his lips.

It was all the encouragement he needed. His body imprisoned her against the soft leather as his mouth plundered hers. He moved lower, his lips seeking her neck, her ears, the straight, hard ridge of her collarbone.

His hand skimmed her side, slid under her shirt, felt the heat of her skin, ran over the contours of her stomach, her ribs and the rise of her breasts. He felt her push urgently against his hand as he cupped a lacy mound and swallowed the gasp she let out as he pushed her bra aside.

It was happening fast. His pulse hammered like a train. His breath was coming in short, sharp pants. But it didn't feel wrong or rushed or awkward. He felt like this was what they'd been destined to do from the beginning, on the balcony that night of the ball. It was almost as if he'd been born to touch her.

And it felt good. Good to feel again. To have lust bubbling in his gut and desire heating his blood. Talking about the tragedies of his life had given him an even greater sense of living. Of making every day, every breath count.

For once he wasn't poor Callum, the widower. Or poor Callum the single dad. Or poor Callum, the father of poor little sick Tom. He was normal. Average. Just another guy. No—not just another guy. He was a hot and virile guy. And Hailey was one hundred per cent into him. He hadn't asked for her pity. And she hadn't given him any.

So what if she had a truckload of baggage? That they

could never be together? Her hands were on him. Touching him, wanting him. Her lips were plastered to his, her tongue dancing an erotic tango. Nothing mattered right now other than this rare moment of indulgence. It was about him and her. About male and female. Two consenting adults moving to a rhythm as old as time.

Hailey felt Callum's hand push her skirt down, his hand on her bare thigh where it met the curve of her bottom, but still she wanted more. She'd never felt such an intense attraction to a man—ever—and she wanted it all. At once. She wanted to be part of him.

She grabbed the back of his shirt and pulled it over his head. He ducked out of it and she tossed it away. In seconds his smooth skin was laid bare to her touch. She wasted no time. He was warm and vital. His muscles contracted beneath her fingernails and she grabbed his buttocks, kneading them, grinding herself against him.

After a year of struggling through the darkness, of grieving and holding it all in and doubting herself professionally and as a woman most of all, Callum's passion was a revelation. It was wonderful to just feel for once. Not to have to think. Or be sad. Or have her memories and her second-guessing driving her mad. Isolating her from life.

His lips on hers, his hand skimming her knickers, pushing up her shirt, pulling aside her other bra cup, exposing her breasts—it all felt so right. Suddenly she wasn't being tiptoed around, being given knowing, sympathetic looks. She was being treated like a desirable woman. Not with kid gloves but with rough, urgent hands that wanted more. And it felt great.

And at this moment it didn't matter that he was still in love with his wife. That he had a little boy. That they worked together. That they weren't possible. None of the flashing lights mattered. None of his baggage mattered. This wasn't about long term. About tomorrow. This was about here and now. About being wanted and desired.

Her hands found their way to his fly. There was no thought to her movements now. She was moving purely on instinct, fuelled by passion. Passion that had been dulled by a train wreck of a relationship and dampened by grief for too long. She heard him moan and any reservations she may have been able to dredge up disappeared as the first button of his fly popped easily at her touch.

And it would have led heaven knew where had not, at the precise moment Callum's mouth closed over a nipple and her back arched, Tom let out a blood-curdling scream.

CHAPTER SIX

CALLUM pulled away abruptly. It took a few seconds for his nerve endings to deliver the impulses to his brain to realise that something was wrong with Tom.

Something was wrong with Tom.

And he was here, getting naked with Hailey? What was he doing? He was Tom's father. Tom needed him. He pushed himself off her. Somewhere he vaguely thought about his shirt but he was moving without any conscious thought, doing up his fly, backing out of the room.

Hailey lay stunned on the lounge in a dishevelled heap, trying to gather her thoughts, get up to speed with what had just happened. Her chest heaved and her breath actually hurt. Reality invaded. Sanity returned. *Tom.* Tom had screamed.

She sat up, pulling her skirt down, shifting her bra back to its rightful place, adjusting her shirt, her heart still beating a crazy tattoo. She finger-combed her hair, licked her lips, savoured the trace of Callum she tasted there. *Oh, God, what the hell had just happened?*

Callum met a hysterical Tom halfway to his bedroom and swept him up into his arms. 'Tommy! What's wrong?'

'My ear. My ear,' Tom sobbed, his hand clutching at his right ear. 'There's something walking in my ear.'

Callum, his pulse pounding through his head, hugged Tom to his chest in a brief, hard embrace. A bug in the ear he could handle. For a moment, in his sluggish lust-drugged brain, he thought the hounds of hell had paid a visit.

'Get it out, get it out,' Tom cried, shaking his head from side to side.

Callum kissed Tom's forehead. 'OK, Tommy. OK.'

He strode into the lounge room, Tom still grasping the side of his head.

'What is it?' Hailey asked, jumping up from the chair. 'Is he OK?'

'Seems like he has an insect in his ear,' Callum said. 'Can you hold him while I get my auroscope and some oil?'

'Of course,' she said breathily, holding out her arms.

Callum transferred Tom into Hailey's waiting arms, his gaze lingering for a second on the swollen fullness of her lips. They exchanged a heated look. He knew he'd be inside her now if they hadn't been interrupted. *How could he have let things get so out of hand?*

'Ow, ow, ow,' Tom cried, pressing his ear hard as he clung to Hailey's neck.

'It's OK, baby,' Hailey crooned, sitting back down on the chair behind her. 'Wont be long now. Daddy will get it out.' Tom writhed on her lap and she held him tight, rocking him slowly, dropping kisses on his forehead.

'It's scratching. It's scratching,' he wailed.

'I know. I know,' she whispered. She'd never had an insect in her ear but she'd nursed a couple of patients who had, and they'd described it as a truly awful experience.

The insect's tiny movements were magnified a hundred-fold because of the proximity to the eardrum. A noise that would normally need a powerful microphone to hear suddenly sounded like a set of bongo drums going off inside the head. There were plenty of old wives' tales about people who had been driven mad by insects in the ear, and if Tom's frantic movement was any indication, she could see why.

Callum flicked on the main lights as he returned with an auroscope, some long-necked angled forceps, a bottle of olive oil and an eyedropper.

'OK, Tom. Let me have a look in your ear.'

Hailey sat Tom so he was straddling her lap, his face pressed into her chest, his head turned slightly so Callum had easy access to his son's right ear. Callum inserted the funnel-shaped earpiece into Tom's ear canal and looked through the magnified viewfinder. The light of the auroscope shone straight down, illuminating everything.

'Oh, yeah. I see it. A little black bug.'

Tom cried some more, rubbing his face into Hailey's shirt.

'Lie down, Tom—let's get that bug out.'

'Put your head on my lap, sweetie,' Hailey suggested, and she helped get Tom into position. 'Lie very, very still.'

Callum filled the eyedropper with olive oil and gently dripped it into Tom's ear. Tom whimpered as the warm oil oozed inside.

'It's OK, Tom,' Hailey soothed, stroking his forehead. 'It'll just feel a little strange.'

Callum refilled the eyedropper and squirted some more in. The object was to drown the insect or at least weigh its legs down with a viscous substance, thus preventing it from moving around. The oil immediately alleviating the pain of seemingly having the percussion section of an orchestra playing at full throttle in his son's head.

Callum was hoping he wouldn't have to use the angled forceps to remove the insect and as they watched, the black bug floated out of Tom's ear canal on a surge of olive oil.

'Hey—there it is!' Callum removed the offending bug, grabbing some tissues out of the box on the coffee-table and placing it on one of them. 'We got it, Tommy. It's out.'

Tom sniffled. 'Can I look?'

Callum used another tissue to absorb the oil puddled in Tom's ear. He helped him up, holding the tissue in place to catch the remainder of the oil as it ran out.

Tom looked at the small black bug. 'What sort of beetle is it, Daddy?'

'Looks like a stinkbug to me,' Callum mused.

'Can I take it for show and tell?'

Callum and Hailey laughed. 'Sure. We'll put it in a specimen pot.'

Tom crawled onto his father's lap and snuggled into his chest. They all sat for a few moments, basking in the after-glow of another crisis averted.

'Daddy,' Tom said, sitting up. 'How come you don't have a shirt on?'

Callum glanced at Hailey. It was hard to believe now that she had pulled it off him not even ten minutes ago. 'It was hot,' he said.

Hailey looked away but not before Callum saw the rise of colour in her cheeks. *Very hot.*

'Ooh, can I have a hot chocolate, please, Daddy?'

Callum laughed, well used to Tom's fluid style of con-versation and short attention span. Normally he would have said no. He'd have awarded Tom full points for trying but he still would have said no. But Tom's scream had given him such a fright he was prepared to indulge his son a little. Tom had, after all, saved him from himself. 'Okay. But then straight to bed.'

'Hailey, too.'

'Oh, I don't know, Tom. It's getting late. I think I might go home.' She didn't really want to hang around and witness their domestic bliss. Her brain was overloaded with enough images to decipher, not least Callum's still bare, very sexy chest—she didn't need any more. She really should go. Think herself lucky that things were halted before they'd gone too far.

'Ple-e-ease, Hailey,' Tom pleaded. 'Please.'

Hailey stared at his earnest little face. She shouldn't. She'd already overstepped way too many lines tonight. Falling asleep with him had been her first. She had a feeling that Tom would all too easily wheedle his way into her heart. God knew, his father was certainly making inroads. Together they were a dangerous team. But she did have him to thank for bringing their hang-the-consequences passion to a screaming halt.

'OK. Just this once.'

They all adjourned to the kitchen. Callum, still shirtless, placed Tom on the central bench and clattered around to find what he needed, keeping up a constant patter with Tom. Anything to keep his mind off what had almost happened in the lounge room.

Hailey watched them together, laughing and chatting, plainly adoring each other, obviously a happy family unit. The two musketeers. She'd been here before. Teetering on the edge of something wonderful, on the brink of inclusion, only to discover when the chips were down that there wasn't any room for her. Callum was still in love with his wife, the wonderful Annie, and she'd be foolish in the extreme to set herself up to play second fiddle again.

They drank their hot chocolate in the kitchen, Tom sitting on the counter, his legs swinging as if he was holding court. Hailey and Callum leaned their hips against the benches, both grateful for the egocentricity of a six-year-old with a milk moustache. Tom didn't notice their distraction or lack of enthusiasm.

Half an hour later Callum bundled Tom off to bed. After a bug hunt in his room revealed no more predators waiting to acquaint themselves with his eardrum, Tom was content to put his head down.

Callum stroked his son's forehead as he drifted off to sleep. Everything that was important to him was right here in this room. It was imperative to focus on that. 'Thank you,' he whispered.

Hailey was gathering her things together when Callum re-entered the lounge room. He stood in the doorway and watched her, not sure what to say now they were alone. One thing was certain, they sure couldn't leave it like it was. 'You're leaving.'

Hailey looked at him. 'I think that's best.'

'I'm sorry about earlier. I don't know what happened. How it got so out of hand so…quickly.'

She shrugged. 'Melancholy. We've been through the mill a bit, you and me. '

It hadn't felt very melancholic to him. 'Is that it? Is that all?' It wasn't wise, it wasn't what he needed—but he wanted her anyway.

She sat on the lounge, staring at her lap. Of course it wasn't. But what other explanation could there be as to how could things have got so serious in a week? OK, yes, she had known at the ball that he was something special. But that had been a reaction to his sheer physicality.

What she had felt tonight, when he'd been talking about Annie and Tom, and yesterday, when he'd helped her with Henry, was an entirely different kettle of fish. That had been much, much worse than a physical pull. There had to be a simple explanation for it.

'What do you want from me, Callum? You want me to admit I'm attracted to you? Fine, I'm attracted to you.' It seemed pointless to deny what they both knew.

He pushed away from the doorframe and made his way closer, only the coffee-table separating them. He sighed. 'The feeling is entirely mutual.'

Hailey nodded. So why did he look as miserable as she felt? 'It's still not going to work.'

'I know. My priority has to be Tom. I'm all he's got.' And the truth was he didn't know how to be a dad to Tom and date at the same time when work and Tom took up all his time before he collapsed into bed in a tired heap at eight-thirty each night. He didn't lead a very thrilling life. What could he offer her?

'Of course he should be. I'd think less of you if he wasn't. Tom still needs you—a lot. Anything we do is going to affect him. It wouldn't be fair on him to start something, to get his hopes up, to have them dashed if it didn't work out. We don't have the freedom to make mistakes and fight and make up and feel our way and then decide it wasn't right to start with. And I've just come through a relationship that, frankly, sucked the soul out of me. I'm a little damaged. Not good relationship material.'

'I think we're a both a little damaged in that depart-ment,' Callum murmured, burying his hands in his pockets.

Hailey nodded. *Right.* She'd be especially foolish to get involved with another man who was still in love with his wife. *His dead wife.* Competing with an ex had been hard enough. Competing against a perfect memory?

She looked up at him. They both had issues that made an involvement problematic. And hadn't they had enough of problematic? Didn't they both deserve a stretch of easy? She stood. 'I'd better go.'

Callum nodded. 'Thank you for tonight. For filling in on such short notice.'

Hailey swallowed, hating the strained formality of his voice. Had it only been an hour ago it had been husky and rich with desire? She picked up her bag. 'You're welcome,' she murmured.

Callum followed her as she limped out, and Hailey was excruciatingly aware of him, of his heat enveloping her in its seductive embrace. She reached for the doorhandle, her hand trembling. The door resisted being opened and she realised it was locked.

'Let me.' Callum reached around her and slowly flipped the lock.

Hailey stood very still while he did it, his body almost pressed against hers. He lifted his hand from the door and placed it on her shoulder, his thumb lightly caressing the skin of her nape. 'I wasn't expecting this, Hailey. I wasn't on the lookout for someone.'

Hailey shut her eyes for a few seconds, almost leaning into his touch, almost resting back against him. She shrugged, looking at him. 'Neither was I.' She dragged in a ragged breath and opened the door. 'Goodnight,' she croaked, escaping into the corridor.

* * *

It was hard, going back to work after her days off. Hailey dreaded the moment she'd run into Callum again. She knew she was going to have to get used to it. That unless she left and went to work somewhere else, she was bound to run into him most days.

But she wasn't going to let her impossible attraction to him dictate the course of her life. She wasn't going to run like she'd run from London. Find another job where they'd never cross paths. Look for another apartment far away from his.

She felt good about working on 2B. Yvonne was a great boss and Rilla and Beth and her father were all close by. She adored her apartment. Rilla had been muttering about selling it and she was seriously considering buying it from her. She wasn't going to let whatever it was between her and Callum derail her life.

It would help, of course, if she could just stop remembering their passionate exchange. The feel of his chest, smooth and warm beneath her palms, taunted her. The taste of his mouth, the shape of his lips, the sound of his deep appreciative groan played relentlessly in her head. The heat of him stayed with her, the smell of him clung to her. The look, the hungry, devouring look he had blasted her with still twisted her insides into knots.

And she was supposed to interact with him like she didn't know these things? Like she didn't remember them? Like there wasn't an erotic movie playing in her head every time she clapped eyes on him?

Good luck!

Surprisingly, though, it was a few days before their paths did cross and not quite in the way Hailey had envisioned.

'Hi, Rosemary, is this the new admission?' Hailey

asked, walking into the medical bay and parking herself at the end of bed eight's cot. Yvonne had asked her to relieve Rosemary so the junior nurse could go to lunch. The ward lights had been dimmed and the curtains pulled for the daily afternoon rest period.

'Yep,' Rosemary confirmed.

'Gosh, he is a skinny minny,' she commented.

Little Timothy Dunbar was three weeks old and had come up from Emergency for intravenous fluids to correct his mild dehydration. He'd been admitted under Callum's team and would have his vomiting and failure to thrive investigated during his stay. It was suspected that the babe had pyloric stenosis.

He was guzzling his bottle like he'd been wandering in a desert. She noted the intricate taping of the IV that had been placed in a scalp vein. With his dehydration venous access had obviously been difficult to find and a scalp vein had been the only option. At least Timothy was bald and they hadn't had to shave any of his hair.

'Yes,' Rosemary agreed, as Timothy finished scoffing his bottle and she sat him on her lap to burp him. 'Nothing wrong with his appetite, though.'

'Here, I'll take him.' Hailey moved closer, holding her arms out. 'You must be starving.'

Timothy chose that moment to prove once and for all that he was heading for the operating theatre. A large fountain of vomit surged from his mouth, covering the metre distance that separated him from Hailey, reaching her uniform in a perfect arc.

Hailey leapt back, her reflexes well honed from years of nursing vomity babies, but unfortunately, this time, not fast enough. Warm, regurgitated milk seeped into her clothes, soaking them and her underwear beneath. She looked down at the mess in dismay as the baby started to cry.

'Shot! Great aim, young Timothy.'

Had she not been covered in baby vomit, Hailey might have felt self-conscious about seeing Callum again for the first time, but the current circumstances weren't conducive to erotic thoughts.

She turned and gave him a quelling look.

He grinned at her. 'Well, I think that confirms our suspicions of pyloric stenosis.'

'Great. A comedian,' she said, reaching for the clean towel on Timothy's bedside cabinet.

Rosemary was looking at a wet Hailey with a horrified expression as she jiggled the fractious Timothy. Hailey had noticed that the junior nurse had been nervous around her since the blocked trachy incident. This was, no doubt, her last straw. Rosemary looked like she expected to be sacked on the spot.

'It's OK, Rosemary. This wasn't your fault. If I had a dollar for every time a patient's thrown up on me, I'd be a rich woman. Why don't you go on to lunch? Dr Craig…' she turned and shot Callum a sarcastic smile '…obviously has time to sit around and be funny. He can hold Timothy while I get changed.'

Callum inclined his head. 'It will be my pleasure. Especially now you appear to be wearing the entire contents of his stomach. I think that makes me safe.'

Callum plucked a still bawling Timothy from Rosemary's lap and cradled him in his arms. 'Shh, Timothy,' he crooned. 'It's OK. You and I are going to have a little chat.' He took the chair that Rosemary had vacated. 'You know it's never polite to throw up over a girl, Timothy. Never.'

Hailey looked down at Callum and rolled her eyes. He winked at her and she shook her head. It was all right for him, he wasn't covered in baby sick. He returned his attention to Timothy and afforded her a view of his downcast head. She remembered how it had felt beneath her hand the other night and her fingers itched to run over it, to feel the velvety stubble tickle her palm again. She threw the towel down on the floor instead, soaking up the puddle on the floor.

'I need a shower. I'll find Joyce.'

Ten minutes later, Hailey had showered and changed into a pair of scrubs. It wasn't ideal but she only had a couple of hours left to make do. Joyce was wheeling her mop and bucket out of the bay as Hailey approached.

'Thanks for mopping up, Joyce.'

'No worries, love.'

Hailey stood at the entrance to the bay and watched Callum still deep in conversation with Timothy. He was sitting on the edge of the low chair, bent forward at the hips with his elbows propped on his thighs, Timothy safely cradled in his outstretched arms. He was slowly rocking him, his big hands supporting Timothy's head and neck expertly.

She'd spent five minutes in the shower trying not to think about Callum Craig's expert hands and what they'd done to her body. *Dear God, pull yourself together!* She strode into the bay annoyed with herself and her one-track thoughts.

'Thank you, Callum,' she said briskly, desperate to maintain a professional façade in front of him when in reality she was wearing underwear she'd washed out in the shower and dried to the best of her ability in a few minutes and her brain was remembering acutely every second of their passionate clinch last week.

'Shh,' Callum scolded quietly, looking up at her.

He tried hard not to do a double-take when he saw her. She was fresh from the shower and in scrubs and looked way more appealing than he'd ever thought possible. What was that old song? Something about women in uniform? He had a sudden urge to retrain as a surgeon.

Her hair was damp around the edges the odd wet tendril fell from a hastily constructed ponytail. Her face was free of make-up and he could see the freckles across her nose that had fascinated him so much at the ball.

Hailey looked down at the efficiently wrapped bundle, looking even smaller in Callum's comparatively giant-like grasp. 'Oh, he's asleep,' she whispered, momentarily caught up in Timothy's button nose and cute bow mouth.

She crouched down in front of Callum and gently stroked Timothy's forehead, being careful to avoid the taping of the scalp vein IV. He looked like a glowworm toy all swaddled in his polar fleece bunny rug, only his head visible.

Callum watched Hailey's face soften. She'd marched over here all businesslike but one look at Timothy's cuteness and she had collapsed like a house of cards. It was the last thing he needed to see. More evidence of how good she was with kids.

He cleared his throat quietly. 'I examined him while you were gone. There's a definite olive shaped mass in his stomach now. I think an ultrasound would be a waste of time. I'm going to see if we can schedule him for OT at the end of this afternoon's list, tomorrow morning's if not.'

Hailey looked up at him. She knew that the lump Callum had felt was the muscles of the pylorus at the distal end of the stomach which had become thickened and enlarged. That made it difficult for food to travel through, and eventually over the first few weeks of life, as in Timothy's case, they become more contracted, resulting in forceful vomiting, failure to thrive and dehydration with sometimes severe electrolyte imbalance.

'Do you want us to fast him?'

Callum nodded. 'I'm pretty sure his stomach is empty now so, yeah, let's fast him and I'll write you up an increase in his IV fluids.'

Hailey nodded. Crouched as she was, their heads were quite close. The urge to touch his hair returned and she clenched her fists.

'I'll see to it.'

Callum nodded. He was reluctant to move. Holding a baby again was nice. It bought back such lovely memories of Tom at this age—before Annie had died, before the leukaemia. Hailey was looking at him with a similar appreciation of such a tiny bundle and he felt that connection with her again. The one he'd felt since the ball.

Hailey was distracted by his hair again. It just begged her to touch it. She shouldn't be but suddenly she was wondering how it would feel rubbing against her skin. Rubbing in places that were entirely inappropriate to be wondering about at work.

She looked away, embarrassed, but not before she'd seen Callum become aware of her blush.

'Hailey? Everything all right?'

She closed her eyes. She couldn't bear the tone of his voice. The one that spoke of shared intimacies. That wasn't how their relationship was going to be.

She looked up, looked him straight in the eyes, and gave a nonchalant shrug despite her heart hammering like made. 'I was just wondering why you wore your hair so short. Are you covering up some premature balding. Or greying?'

Callum laughed. 'None of the above. I made a pact with Tom. When he started to lose his hair, I shaved mine off too.' He shrugged. 'I kind of got used to it. It's low maintenance and I don't have to brush it ever.'

'Oh.' Hailey hadn't thought of that contingency. Of course. It made perfect sense. What else would a father dedicated to his son do?

Callum watched her digest the information and couldn't work out what she was thinking. But he'd hoped they'd get the opportunity to talk again and now was as good a time as any.

'So, we're OK? You and me? You think we can do this? Just be colleagues? It's not going to be weird between us?'

'Of course not.' Even if it killed her, she'd make sure of it.

'Even if the whole time you were away, the whole time I was speaking to an impressionable infant, all I could think about was you in the shower?'

Hailey swallowed as the blast of heat from his bold statement mixed with the heat in her face and she momentarily lost her train of thought. He'd been thinking about her? In the shower? Naked?

And her? What had she been thinking about? Him. OK, maybe not naked but she doubted it would have taken her imagination long to get him that way.

This was clearly insane. They had to put the brakes on. She moved her head closer to him, directing her mouth closer to his ear. 'We've been through this, Callum. Do me a favour, don't think about me in the shower. Don't think about me naked at all. Friends are all we can be.'

Callum sighed. She was right. 'Of course. Friends.'

She nodded and pulled back from his closeness, snatching a big lungful of Callum-infused air as she went. She stood on shaky legs and walked away to arrange Timothy's pre-op care.

Good. They were both on the same page.

CHAPTER SEVEN

LIFE went on. Working together got easier. They were professional around each other but both studiously avoided anything of a personal nature. Two months passed. Due to an unexpected illness, Hailey was offered a seat on the organising committee for the Brisbane General's annual children's picnic. She grabbed it with both hands, investing every spare moment into it, grateful to became absorbed in something other than Callum.

Unfortunately her attraction for Callum hadn't ended. She'd just learnt to file it under 'Some things in life you can't have' and moved on. The younger, more impulsive Hailey would have thrown caution to the winds, but the older, wiser Hailey knew the fall was treacherous. So, he was as sexy as hell and she wanted him. It would pass.

Tom, however, had insinuated himself into her life well and truly. She wasn't sure how it had happened but he seemed to spend quite a few afternoons a week watching cable TV at her place. It had become a sort of routine, one Hailey was enjoying immensely.

Tom would finish his homework and if she wasn't working, his grandmother, who picked him up from school and stayed until Callum got home, would send him to her for an hour or so, always bearing some home-baked goody for them to share.

It was a bitter-sweet time. But not as bad as when she witnessed Callum and Tom together. She often spotted them around the apartment complex, in the lifts or by the pool, and occasionally even at work, when Callum brought Tom into 2B on weekends for his rounds. It tugged at Hailey's heart to observe their easy interaction. Their relationship was everything a father and son's should be. It reminded her of Eric and Paul, and as painful as that was to relive, it helped to keep her focused on not repeating past mistakes.

Hailey was relieved when mid-March finally arrived and the Saturday of the picnic dawned bright and clear. She was nervous and excited in equal measure. The culmination of two months' work was about to unfold and she couldn't wait to see the looks on the children's faces today. But the number of things that could go wrong also weighed on her mind. At least the weather had behaved.

She was out early at the local park with a band of eager volunteers, helping to set up. The annual picnic was part fundraiser and part community service. A way of throwing a little sunshine into the lives of kids—and their families— who were either currently inpatients or had been patients in the past. A way of giving back to the community while raising awareness of the important role the Brisbane General played.

It was a free event. The hospital was able to subsidise the rides, the food and the entertainment largely because most of the attractions had been donated. All money raised from raffles, silent auctions and charitable offerings on the day, both big and small, were channelled directly back into

2B. Many pieces of ward equipment had been bought over the years because of the yearly picnic. Unfortunately, as government budgets grew tighter, only covering the bare necessities, events such as the picnic were vital fundraisers.

By the time eleven o'clock came round and the gates opened, Hailey already felt exhausted. But the excited chatter of children as they streamed past her and the looks on the faces of parents who had left their worries at the gate made the hours of toil, of phone calls, of checking every minute detail, all worthwhile.

There was a true carnival atmosphere. A Ferris wheel dominated the end of the park and, along with a massive merry-go-round, was bound to keep the kids happy all day. Children's music blared from the loudspeakers. Clown doctors were set to wander around, entertaining the kids with jokes and balloon animals.

Stalls with various carnival games were dotted around and she could see the petting zoo was already popular. It felt good looking out on it all, knowing that she had been part of it.

Hailey spent most of the day helping out at one stall or another. On her travels she bumped into a lot of old patients and she stopped to chat with the kids and their families. It was great to see them again and catch up on what had happened after discharge.

A lot of them didn't recognise her thanks to the brilliant face-painting artists they'd employed for the day. Hailey had been done up to look like a cat, a stripy marmalade one, and even Beth had walked straight past her.

At two o'clock, with three hours to go, her father sought her out. 'There you are, darling. Beth said to look for the cat that looks like she's swallowed the cream. You've done a fabulous job,' John Winters commented, kissing his daughter carefully on her blackened nose.

Hailey laughed. 'Well, I didn't do it all by myself, Dad.'

'C'mon, its time for the dunking booth to open. Your mother thought you wouldn't want to miss it.'

'Miss my father and two brothers-in-law getting wet for a good cause? It's going to be the highlight of my day.'

The old adage that it wasn't what you knew but who you knew certainly played out when it came to charity. There was nothing like having the Brisbane General's medical director, a world-renowned surgeon who had separated three sets of conjoined twins, and the emergency department director all lining up for a good dunking. Hailey had known people would pay a high price to see all or any of them dunked and luckily they'd all been good-natured enough to agree.

A crowd had gathered and there was much excitement as John, resplendent in polka-dot boardies and a bright yellow sun shirt, took the first turn. He looked like a canary or, at the very least, a sitting duck.

'There she is, Daddy.'

Hailey knew it was Tom's high little voice even before she homed in on his location. 'Tom,' she said, as the little boy, orchie in tow, launched his body at her legs rugby-tackle style. She absorbed the impact and looked down at him, ruffling his hair.

'I told Daddy you'd be here.'

She smiled down at him and ruffled his hair again. How on earth he could tell it was her when her own sister hadn't recognised her, she didn't know.

'What's new, pussycat?'

The sun was behind Callum as she squinted up at him,

making him appear even more dazzling than usual. He was in baggy denim shorts and a T-shirt that had a tropical sunset decorating his chest. She'd never seen him looking this devastatingly casual. She'd seen him in jeans a few times but never in shorts that revealed the tanned muscularity of his legs covered in light brown hair.

'I haven't heard that one yet today,' she said derisively.

Callum laughed. 'Meow!'

'Is that your dad?' Tom interrupted, pointing at John, who had so far managed to stay on the tiny seat perched over the tank of water, despite several attempts to dethrone him.

'It sure is.' Hailey nodded. 'You want a go?'

Tom nodded his head excitedly and Hailey took his hand.

'OK, folks,' she announced to the crowd, who were booing and taunting John good-naturedly, threatening him with an imminent dunking. 'Tom's turn.'

She handed Tom a ball but it was clear that to be given any chance of success he needed some height.

'Here, Tommy,' Callum said, striding forward and lifting his son onto his hip. 'How's that?'

'I think we could probably make allowances for the boy and have him come a little closer to the target, too,' John said. 'He's only six.'

'Ah, but he's got a good eye, John,' Callum warned with a smile on his face. Hadn't he managed to spot Hailey underneath all that face paint? 'Are you sure you want to risk it?'

John gave a hoot. 'I think I'm pretty safe.'

'Three turns, Tom.' Hailey grinned and nodded at him to go.

The first one fell shy of the target by a good metre.

'Bad luck, Tom,' John called.

Tom looked disappointed but the crowd clapped and

cheered and urged him to try again. His second shot sailed too far to the right.

'Come on, Tom,' John shouted over the top of the crowd. 'You can do better than that.'

Hailey watched as his little chin jutted out determinedly, so like his father, and he squinted at the target. He swung back and threw the ball hard, hitting the mark dead on.

The crowd went wild as the seat gave way and plunged the Brisbane General medical director straight into the water. Callum jumped up and down with Tom as Hailey clapped wildly. She hugged Tom and joined them in their father-son jumping.

'You did it, Tom. You did it.' She laughed.

Callum was aware of every movement of Hailey's body against his. The slide of her breasts against his chest. The bounce of her hair around her shoulders, a stray tendril gliding against the skin of his arm. The feel of her hand in the middle of his back strangely intimate.

He stopped jumping, looking down into her painted face, her freckles obliterated by brown and ginger stripes. She smiled up at him, her soft eyes suiting the elaborate feline mask. Her mouth was painted black too and he couldn't believe that something such a ghastly colour looked so tempting.

They hadn't been this close since that night. The night they'd almost made love on the lounge. He'd made a real effort to keep his distance this last two months. To treat her with the utmost of professional courtesy and respect. And nothing else.

It had been hard. Treating her as one of the team at work wasn't easy when she all too readily invaded his dreams at night. *And there was nothing collegial about them.* Going to work each day and having to edit his thoughts and actions all the time was a strain when in his dreams he was much more daring, took much greater liberties. And, worse, she welcomed them.

Hailey saw the heat warm his grey gaze and pulled away. She faltered slightly before getting her brain back on track. 'Well done, Tom,' she said, ruffling his hair one more time.

They stayed and watched as John got dunked several more times, followed by Gabe, who got away relatively unscathed, and then Luca, who seemed to spend more time in the water than out. She was conscious of Callum's gaze the entire time.

'Oh, no, poor Luca,' Hailey teased as she handed her brother-in-law a towel. 'What a pity Rilla had to work. She would have loved to have seen this.'

'I'm heading back to the General now.' He grinned. 'I suspect she'll get the idea.'

'I think Mum videoed it anyway.'

Luca turned and waved at Penny Winters, who was looking through the viewfinder of her handy cam. He groaned and muttered, '*Dio.*'

Tom tugged on Hailey's hand and she looked down at him.

'Can you come on the Fewwis wheel with me and my dad?'

Hailey smiled, charmed by his mispronunciation. Just about everything to do with Tom charmed her. And, yes, agreeing to join them was hardly keeping a distance from Callum, but it had been two months, and apart from the erotic dreams and the exchange of one very steamy look earlier, they had been very good. Surely they could ease up a little and share one ride on a big wheel?

'I love the Ferris wheel.' She grinned.

They stopped on the way and bought Tom some blue fairy floss. 'He's tried all the other colours.' Callum grimaced.

Hailey cocked an eyebrow at him. 'That's a lot of sugar.'

'I wouldn't ordinarily but he does love it and, well...it's a picnic.' He shrugged sheepishly.

Hailey rolled her eyes at him. 'Soft touch,' she teased quietly.

Thankfully there wasn't a queue and they were ushered straight into one of the open gondolas. Tom sat next to Hailey on one side and Callum took the seat opposite, his legs stretched out in front of him, perilously close to hers. She'd been nervous about what they were going to say to each other but she needn't have been. Tom took centre stage and she was happy to let him chat away, too conscious of Callum in her peripheral vision.

Tom shared his fairy floss with her and chatted about the picnic and what his favourite parts of the day had been. Food seemed to feature a lot.

'Three snow cones?' She looked at Callum.

'There were a couple of years when he rarely ate enough to keep a sparrow alive. It's good to see his appetite back. I don't mind indulging him on special days.'

Hailey nodded slowly. Fair enough. She hadn't thought about it from that perspective before. She knew anorexia was a major problem with chronically ill children and caused a great deal of stress and anxiety for their parents. She guessed that in situations like that you didn't care what your child ate as long as they ate something.

The Ferris wheel went round at a lazy pace, giving its riders many more revolutions than they would have had at a normal carnival. The breeze ruffled her hair, lifting it off the back of her neck, and she helped it further by piling it up on top of her head and holding it there, allowing the breeze to cool her neck.

The sunny day was quite warm and it felt heavenly to be sitting in the shade of the gondola's umbrella, complete with Mother Nature's air-conditioning. She'd been up late all week with last-minute preparations and up at the crack of dawn today, and having a few minutes' respite had alerted her to how weary she felt. She shut her eyes and let Tom's chatter wash over her.

Callum took the opportunity to observe her. The face paint should have looked ridiculous on a grown woman but it didn't. It made her look…exotic. Feline and female in the way cats often were, slinking around, twitching their tails, weaving in and out of your legs, rubbing against you, purring contentedly, urging you to stroke them.

With her hair out of the way he admired the line of her neck, bare of jewellery, her olive skin tantalising. He remembered how good it had felt to kiss her there. Her T-shirt fitted her chest snugly, stretching across her bust, emphasising its fullness, the V-neckline revealing a hint of cleavage.

She was wearing cargo pants that stopped just below her knees. They fit her hips and legs but he could see the bunching at her waist where the pants were obviously too big. He imagined she had that problem a lot with her small waist flowing out to fuller hips.

Tom started to chat about his grandparents taking him to the 'Gold Coat' and Hailey opened her eyes. They came slowly into focus, Callum's features becoming sharp and distinct, his grey gaze steady. She stared unblinkingly, mesmerised by what she saw there. No doubt the most fascinating eyes she'd ever known. How easy would it be to get lost in those eyes? How easy would it be to throw caution to the winds and cross the line they'd drawn in the sand?

'Isn't that exciting, Hailey?'

She held Callum's gaze for a moment longer before dragging it away and turning her attention to Tom. 'Yes, darling.' She used the endearment without even thinking about it, giving his skinny arm a squeeze.

'How long is he going for?' she asked Callum conversationally.

He sighed. 'A few days.'

Hailey frowned at the heavy sigh. 'You don't sound too thrilled about it.'

He shook his head. 'No, it's fine.'

Hailey narrowed her eyes, sensing Callum's hesitation. 'But?' She looked down at Tom, who had twisted around in his seat, his attention fully taken by the gondolas behind. 'Don't you get on?' she mouthed quietly as she took the precariously dangling torch from a compliant Tom lest it drop and land on someone's head in a gondola below.

She'd met Margo, Annie's mother, and had been thoroughly impressed. But who knew what boiled beneath the surface? Maybe they blamed him for Annie's death? For Tom's illness? Maybe they'd never approved of him?

'We get on fine. They're great. I don't know what I'd do without them.'

Hailey nodded slowly. 'So why do I still sense a "but"?'

Callum stared out to the side. They'd stopped at the top as the gondolas below were emptied one by one. He could see the Brisbane General from here. 'They try to protect him too much. They panic over the merest sniffle. I understand why but I don't need that. I can imagine the worst perfectly well on my own without both of them worrying over a paper cut or a sore throat. I'm afraid that going to the beach might not be as fun as Tom is hoping if they don't let him do anything.'

Ah. 'I guess that's their job—to worry.'

'I know that. And I understand. Tom is their one remaining connection to Annie and I would never deny them that, but they need to give him room to be a kid.'

The carriage descended a level and then stopped again, swinging slightly. Callum took a deep breath of warm air, dropping his head back, allowing the sun to warm his face. He was enjoying this. They hadn't spoken in anything other than a professional capacity for two months. It was nice to not talk shop with her.

'I can't believe what a glorious day it is. Don't get too many of these in Melbourne.'

'Is that why you moved' she asked, observing the tanned column of his throat.

Callum shook his head. 'Partly. Annie's parents had always been going to retire to Queensland and I knew they wouldn't if we stayed.' He shrugged, opening his eyes and looking directly at her. 'It was time we made a move. Tom had finished his treatments and his condition had stabilised and…we needed to get away…from the memories and the…bad things. We needed a fresh start.'

'We or you?' she asked gently.

He gave her a grudging smile. 'Me, I guess, most of all. I think Annie would have approved, though. She always loved the sunshine state. I know Margo and Keith were over the moon. I think it was best for all of us. I think I made the right decision.'

Hailey heard the edge of doubt infect his confident words. He looked so isolated, so alone. It was something she'd often seen on Paul's face. The fact that the buck stopped at him, that he alone was responsible, that there was no one else to lean on. She reached forward and gave his knee a pat. 'Well, for what it's worth, I think you did. You're well liked at the hospital and Tom seems to love it here.'

The urge to cover her hand with his was strong but she moved it away before it could happen. Her words did help. 'Yes, he loves his new home.' Due in large part to his afternoon visits to Hailey's.

Tom returned his attention to them and they chatted about lighter things as the Ferris wheel inched closer to the ground until it was their time to get off.

Callum's pager beeped as they alighted. 'Sorry, I'll just get this,' he said, pulling his mobile phone out of his pocket.

Hailey took Tom over to watch the clown doctors and they were both giggling when Callum joined them. 'Damn, I have to go to the General. There's a baby they need me to see.'

'Oh, Daddy, I don't want to go yet. I still haven't had a go on the merry-go-round.'

'Tom, I'm sorry, we have to go.'

'Can't you go and I stay?'

'You can't stay here by yourself, Tom.'

'I'm not by myself,' he said, sliding his hand into Hailey's. 'I'm with Hailey.'

Hailey looked at Tom, who was looking up at her with pleading eyes, and felt herself melt. 'How long will you be, do you think?' She'd promised to help clean up afterwards. Not to mention she'd also promised herself not to get involved with the Craig men. A promise she'd already broken when she kept opening her door to Tom.

Callum looked at their joined hands and felt as if he'd

been punched in the solar plexus. It looked so right. He shouldn't encourage this. He looked at her sheepishly. 'Hopefully only an hour at most.' After today he really must start to curtail Tom's time with Hailey.

Hailey capitulated with a light sigh. 'OK, then.'

Tom jumped up and down and hugged her legs. Callum grinned at her.

'Yeah, yeah,' she said, rolling her eyes. 'Just go.'

Tom didn't seem concerned by his father's absence at all as he ran around like a mad thing from stall to stall. Hailey felt exhausted, just watching him. The exuberance of childhood or a lethal mix of preservatives from the many and varied sugar-filled treats he'd consumed?

An hour passed. An hour and a half passed. People started to leave. The picnic was shutting at five and the organisers were looking forward to getting the cleaning up over and done with so they could have a well-deserved rest and a quiet celebration. The day had been a roaring success.

It was nearly five when Tom staggered off the merry-go-round after five turns. He looked dizzy and more pale than usual. He looked at Hailey and said. 'I don't feel too good.'

Hailey wasn't surprised, with all that sugar in his system. She knelt down to give him a sympathetic hug when he suddenly bent over and dry-retched. Hailey picked him up and put him down next to a nearby bin and rubbed his back as he emptied the contents of his stomach. Luckily the park was nearly deserted now and he got to disgrace himself in relative privacy.

She wiped his mouth with a serviette she had stashed in her pocket. She made a note to tell Callum there was indulgence and then sheer gluttony! She pulled Tom close to her. He felt all floppy and his forehead was hot against her neck.

A prickle of alarm skittered down her spine. She pulled him away. 'Are you OK?' she asked, giving him a little shake as he shut his eyes.

'Feel really sick,' Tom whispered, his head flopping back against her shoulder. 'Where's orchie?'

Hailey felt a full-on surge of alarm rip through her system as she pressed his 'security blanket' into his weak grasp. Oh, God. God, no. It couldn't be happening again. She picked him up, her legs charging towards the exit, her mind in full catastrophe mode, thinking too quickly to actually form any cohesive plan. All she knew was she had to get him to a hospital.

What if he was relapsing? She stopped. Put him down. Did a quick check for bruises on his limbs and torso. There were a couple on his legs she hadn't noticed earlier. Her heart slammed in her chest. She picked him up again and continued on her way. His chances if he relapsed were awful. It was imperative she get him to medical help immediately.

She looked from side to side as she went, trying to think straight while the London disaster played over and over in her mind. Eerily similar echoes of that time taunted her. Tom felt like a boneless sack in her arms. She remembered how floppy Eric had been when his father had tried to wake him, how she had dismissed Eric's tiredness as exhaustion after a big day. She wouldn't do the same with Tom. She wouldn't drop the ball with another little boy.

'I'm going to the hospital,' she called to one of the committee members, not breaking stride, not even knowing who it was, not caring about the edge of panic in her voice. She should feel guilty, leaving everyone else to clean up, but nothing was more important than getting Tom to hospital. Getting him to a doctor. To Luca. To his father.

Callum. Oh, God, she had to let Callum know. She pulled her mobile out of her pocket and dialled his number, still steaming ahead. It went to his message bank. 'Damn it!' she cursed, waiting for the tone. 'Callum? It's Hailey. Something's wrong with Tom. Meet me at Emergency.' She hit the 'end' button and was pleased to see her car was not far away now.

Tom murmured sleepily as she gently placed him in the seat and buckled him up. Her hand shook as she turned the ignition key, her pulse pounding in her head, the thought of Eric's lifeless little body taunting her, scaring her, sickening her.

She forced herself to drive with care to the General, even though every instinct told her to put her foot down to get around the sudden influx of weekend drivers afflicting the road. To run the orange lights that littered her path. To take right of way from people who didn't realise the emergency that was unfolding in her car. The trip took ten minutes and each one felt like an age.

She screeched to a halt in the emergency parking bay outside the General's emergency department, running around the other side and taking Tom out, waking him in the process.

'Where are we?' Tom murmured looking around, clutching his torch.

'At the hospital, baby,' she whispered, her voice feeling almost strangled by the lump in her throat. She prayed hard to all the deities she'd ever learned about at school. *Please, don't let anything happen to this dear little boy.*

She left both car doors open as she strode inside, forgetting about the paint that covered her face, trying to curb her panic, trying to think clearly so she could articulate what she needed.

'Hails?'

Hailey almost fainted from sheer relief when Rilla called her name.

'Oh, thank God,' she half sobbed, passing Tom over to her sister. 'Is Luca here? It's Tom. He has a fever and he's been vomiting and there's some bruising on his legs. You have to get Luca.'

Rilla looked at an increasingly bright-eyed and bushy-tailed Tom giving her a very cheeky grin. He looked like he'd been sleeping but apart from that he didn't look too sick to her. Hailey, on the other hand looked almost beside herself. She may have been covered in thick face paint but it didn't disguise the agitated fidgeting of her hands or the worried shifting from foot to foot.

'Rilla! Please. Don't just stand there. He needs his temp taken. He needs a full blood count. He needs a doctor, damn it!'

Rilla looked at her sister. She knew where this was coming from and she knew it would require delicate treatment. 'Come on, I'll go and get Luca,' she said calmly. 'What about Callum?'

'I left him a message.'

Rilla nodded, making a mental note to page Callum after speaking with Luca. Heaven only knew what kind of a panicked message Hailey had left. She ushered her sister into a cubicle and pulled the curtain. 'Sit up here, Tom,' she said, plonking him on the narrow examination bed. 'I'm going to take your temperature, OK?'

'With an ear one or under my arm?' Tom asked.

'An ear one,' Rilla confirmed with a grin. She placed the tympanic thermometer into Tom's ear canal, laughing at his funny face, and waited for the beep.

'What is it?' Hailey demanded, pacing the small cubicle area.

'Thirty seven point five,' Rilla said.

Hailey sat down, feeling physically ill. 'He does have a fever.'

Rilla gave her sisters shoulder a squeeze. 'It's hardly raging, Hails.'

Hailey looked at her sharply. What was the matter with her? Didn't she realise how quickly children could die? Because she did. Rilla was an experienced emergency nurse, she must know this stuff. 'Get Luca,' Hailey ordered.

'Hails.'

'I want blood tests.' Hailey tried really hard not to shout or sound too frantic so she didn't scare Tom, but she was caught on a déjà vu treadmill and already things in her mind had escalated to tragic proportions.

Rilla left the cubicle and came back with Luca. Hailey was pacing again while Tom was shining his torch at the ceiling and making shadow puppets.

'Hi, Tom,' Luca greeted the boy, glancing at Hailey and then at his wife.

'Hello,' Tom said, not looking away from his torchlight fun.

'What's going on, Hailey?' Luca asked gently.

'I think he might be…' she looked at Tom, not paying any attention to the adults. 'R. E. L. A. P. S. I. N. G. He needs a full blood work-up.'

Luca looked at Rilla again. 'I think we'd need Callum's permission to go ahead and do that.'

The curtain opened abruptly, making a harsh scraping noise. 'Tom!'

'Daddy!' Tom jumped up from his reclining position, running along the length of the gurney and throwing himself into his father's arms.

A breathless Callum hugged him tight, relieved to see that there didn't seem to be too much wrong with him at all. Hailey's message had scared the hell out of him and a dozen worst case scenarios had stormed through his mind as he had run down the fire escape two stairs at a time and bolted to Emergency.

'Daddy, you're squeezing me.' Tom giggled.

Callum relaxed his grip a little and kissed his son's forehead. 'What's going on here?' Callum demanded. Hailey looked wild-eyed, her hands twisting together, opening her mouth to say something and then stopping again.

Rilla jumped in. 'Hailey was a bit concerned that Tom was coming down with something.'

'He has a fever, Callum,' Hailey said, her voice tense with worry. 'He vomited. He has a fever. There's bruising on his legs.'

Callum's pulse accelerated as her poorly leashed panic started to infect him. He knew what she was saying. He tightened his arms around Tom again, ignoring his protests as he inspected his son's legs. He sighed. 'Those bruises are from yesterday, Hailey.' He hugged Tom some more. 'What's his temp?' he asked Rilla.

'Thirty-seven five.'

Callum felt relief flood his system, his heart banging so loudly he thought his chest was about to explode. He looked at Hailey and wanted to wring her neck for frightening him so much.

'Hailey.' He looked at her over Tom's head the anxiety creasing her brow obvious. He sighed. 'You scared the hell out of me.'

Hailey blinked at the anxiety in his voice. She hadn't meant to. Tom was sick, she'd had to get him to hospital.

Rilla looked from Callum to Hailey. They obviously needed to talk. 'Tom, why don't Luca, you and I go and find you a sticker?' Rilla suggested. 'We have some around here somewhere.'

'Yay! I love 'tickers,' Tom said eagerly, scrambling down from his father's almost constrictive embrace, blissfully unaware of the tension in the cubicle. He took Rilla's hand eagerly.

'Go easy,' Rilla said quietly to Callum, nailing him with a fierce look before flicking the curtains aside and letting an eager Tom pull her along, chatting happily about stickers and the picnic.

Callum watched them go, encouraged by his son's bright chatter and his energetic skipping. Rilla's words turned over in his head.

'Are you sure Tom…?'

'He's fine,' Callum said gently, turning back to face her.

Hailey felt tears well in her eyes as his quiet insistence ripped through her anxiety. Her panic started to recede, the awful sense of déjà vu, holding her in its clutches, released her. Rilla, Luca and Callum weren't concerned. No one seemed worried. She could hear Tom's bright laughter and started to realise what she'd done.

'I'm sorry, I just thought… He vomited and was really floppy and…'

Callum covered the distance between them and crouched

down in front of the chair she was sitting on. 'He had enough sugar to run a rum distillery,' he said patiently.

Hailey nodded, the lump in her throat getting bigger by the second. Sugar and merry-go-rounds didn't mix. The bruises were old. She'd made a terrible mistake. 'Of course… I…'

He rubbed his neck. She was looking so mortified. So isolated. He put his arms around her shoulders and pulled her close. She'd given herself a huge fright too and his instincts told him she needed comfort, not a reprimand.

'I'm sorry, Callum,' she said into his neck. 'You have every right to be angry with me.'

Callum pulled back slightly. 'I'm not angry with you. You did frighten the life out of me, though,' Callum said, running his hand over the stubble of his hair. 'I understand where this is coming from, Hailey, I do, but I get enough of this kind of panic from Annie's parents.'

Hailey nodded, swallowing the lump in her throat. He rubbed his hands up and down her arms as he spoke, a gesture she found immeasurably comforting.

'I'm on tenterhooks every day as it is. I have nightmares about him relapsing. I…' He looked around for the right word and decided the English language didn't possess one that could do any justice to his overwhelming feelings of impotency. 'I hate how out of control of all this I am. But I'm trying to give him a normal life. He's not Eric, Hailey.'

Hailey nodded, feeling her chest constrict as the enormity of the panic she'd created sunk in. Stupid, stupid, stupid. She'd let what had happened with Eric override her clinical judgement. Let it blind her to what had been in front of her all along—a kid with too much sugar and boyhood exuberance on board. She felt foolish. 'I know,' she whispered, leaning into the comforting stroke of his hands. 'I'm sorry.'

'Maybe it's best if you and Tom don't see so much of each other.' He didn't want to do this to punish her but Tom and Hailey had been spending a lot of time together and he didn't know if he could survive another of those calls.

Hailey nodded. Tom had wormed his way into her heart. The dread she'd experienced that afternoon when she'd thought he was sick had been almost crippling. Maybe a little distance from him was a good idea.

'I'm going to take Tom home.'

Hailey looked into the calm grey pools of his eyes and saw his withdrawal. Paul's had been like that. She averted her gaze, unable to stand the distance she saw in Callum's. She stared down at her hands, knowing he was right, hoping he wouldn't see how much it hurt. 'Of course.'

'See you next week,' he said gently. Part of him wanted to linger, to take her back in his arms. The other part wanted to go to Tom and hug him close.

He chose Tom.

CHAPTER EIGHT

HAILEY WOKE to pounding at her door on Sunday night. She looked at her bedside clock with bleary eyes. Nine. She hadn't slept a wink last night after the incident with Tom and had finally fallen into the black abyss of sleep from sheer weariness about an hour previously.

She sat up, knocking something to the floor, the room in darkness except for the flicker from the television set. She switched the lamp on, trying to orientate herself as she squinted at the insult to her eyes. Her head felt like it was full of cotton wool.

The bed was strewn with several DVDs, the remote, headphones, photo albums and several scrunched-up discarded tissues she'd used to wipe away the flood of tears that she hadn't seemed able to stop since yesterday. The incident with Tom had bought back memories of Eric's battle for life and Paul's betrayal. It had been an emotional time.

The door was pounded on again and she threw the duvet back, covering most of the mess. Who would be calling at nine o'clock on a Sunday night? She padded to the door and looked through the peephole. Callum? Her heart slammed against her rib cage. She looked again. It was definitely Callum—her guilty conscience hadn't just conjured him up.

She fumbled with the handle as she opened the door. 'Callum?'

He looked terrible. His jaw was dusted with dark stubble, looking rough and scratchy, almost the exact opposite of the velveteen stubble that covered his scalp. His clothes looked like they'd been hastily thrown on, his creased, collared shirt untucked with the buttons done up wrongly. His grey eyes looked troubled. Stormy.

Callum's gaze devoured her from her tousled hair and sleepy eyes to the crease on her face obviously from her bedclothes. 'I woke you up.'

'It's OK,' she dismissed.

Now he was there, he wasn't sure how to start. He had acted on impulse, not giving a lot of thought to what he was going to say. 'I dreamt about Annie,' he said after a moment. 'I haven't dreamt about her in years.'

Hailey gazed at him for a few moments and nodded. 'Where's Tom?'

'At the coast with his grandparents.'

'Of course. I forgot.' She nodded again, holding his troubled gaze. 'Come in. I'll make us a cup of tea,' she said quietly, opening the door further and standing aside.

He followed her through to the kitchen, watching her wordlessly from the doorway as she padded around in her bare feet. She flicked on the kettle, took some mugs out of an overhead cupboard, placed teabags in the cups, spooned sugar into them.

She was wearing a white singlet with shoestring straps that didn't quite meet the waistband of her long striped cotton pyjama bottoms. He could see her belly button and her untethered breasts bounce with each movement. 'I owe you an apology. I didn't mean it about not seeing Tom again.'

Hailey gripped the kitchen counter. 'No.' She shook her head. 'You were right. I overreacted.'

He pushed away from the doorway and moved to stand on the other side of the bench. 'And I knew where that was coming from. I know how much Eric's death affected you. I was just…a little…thrown.'

Hailey didn't want him to apoligise. She'd spent the last day castigating herself for yesterday's debacle. She'd alarmed Callum unnecessarily. Callum, who lived every day under the cloud of Tom's possible relapse. And she'd made a fool of herself in front of Rilla and Luca, not to mention setting her confidence back months.

After Eric she had doubted her skills, her ability, her clinical judgement—had even contemplated giving up nursing altogether. But her family had convinced her to work on 2B and slowly her faith had been restored.

Until yesterday.

The kettle boiled and then switched itself off, and she poured their tea automatically. She picked both mugs up and carried them through to the lounge, conscious of Callum's gaze on her back. She placed them on the coffee-table and took a seat.

Callum was too restless to sit. He didn't know why he'd come. What he was doing there. He'd just known he'd had to come. He prowled around the room, commenting on the view over the Brisbane River, touching her books, picking up the trophy she'd won at sports day when she'd been nine, admiring her CD collection.

He turned to her and shrugged. 'I don't know why I'm here.'

Hailey sipped her tea. 'It's OK.' She supposed it'd become clear to him sooner or later. All she knew was she was glad.

He picked up some framed photos, snapshots of her childhood, but he didn't appear to really be taking them in. Not until he picked up the last one, anyway.

'You put it in a frame?' Callum turned round and held out the photo he'd discovered forgotten in the pages of her book.

Hailey paused, the mug of tea halfway to her mouth. She nodded. Her gaze took in the photo again. Took in the happy faces of the people who all seemed like strangers to her now. Back when no dark clouds had hung on her horizon and life had been bright and breezy.

She put the mug down without taking a sip. 'Yes.'

Callum stared into the smiling faces, none of them aware of the whammy that had lurked round the corner. He remembered those years when he and Tom had been indomitable. 'He looks like a nice kid.'

She swallowed. 'He was.' It still hurt to use the past tense.

'They look happy. You all look happy.' Paul looked as if he'd won the lotto. The look of a man secure in his life and sure of his world. Callum had a picture of Annie and himself and Tom as a baby just before Annie's diagnosis. They'd both looked like that. So...so damn cocky.

Hailey shut her eyes, a lump lodging in her throat. 'They were. We were.'

Callum looked at her. 'I'm sorry. I didn't mean...'

She opened her eyes and looked at him. 'It's OK.'

She watched him replace the frame gently, reverently. He pushed his hands into the front pockets of his jeans and rocked on his heels.

There was more silence while he rocked and she slowly sipped her tea. She couldn't explain it but there was a strange tension between them tonight. A vibe. He obviously didn't know what was going on inside him and she could sense his confusion. Heaven knew, she felt just as uncertain.

Yesterday's incident had shifted the dynamic between them. It should have damaged them but somehow, with him here in front of her, it seemed it had done the opposite. It didn't feel as if he was there to blame her. It felt like he was there to connect with her. Even if he wasn't sure why.

'This is the first night I've spent away from Tom since he was born.'

Hailey let the statement settle for a while between them. 'That must be weird for you.'

He stalked over to where she had placed his mug and picked it up. 'Yes.' He brought the hot drink to his lips and took a sip. He looked into the murky depths of the tea, the weight of her gaze heavy on his skin. It tasted so…bland.

He looked up at her. 'I'm sorry, do you have something…stronger.'

Hailey blinked. *This was serious.* 'I have some beer left over from when Gabe and Beth last came over for tea.'

'Beer would be great.' Callum breathed a sigh of relief.

Hailey rose. She retrieved a long-necked beer from the fridge, cracked the lid and was acutely aware of the frostiness against her fingers as she passed it wordlessly to Callum.

'Thanks,' he said, taking a long drag. The bitter taste swirled around his tongue and he felt the muscles in his shoulders relax a notch. He took another mouthful as he thought about words he could use to make sense of his intrusion.

'I've been thinking a lot since yesterday.'

'I panicked.'

He ignored her, running his finger over the frosty beer label. 'I picked up the phone a hundred times to call you.'

'You didn't have to.'

'Yes, I did. I shut you out.'

She shrugged. 'I overreacted. I scared you.'

He gave her a half-smile. Yes, she had. 'I think you scared yourself more.'

Hailey shivered, remembering the moment of blind panic, the crippling sense of déjà vu. 'I should have used my eyes, my…skills instead of allowing something from my past override my common sense.'

'Eric's death wasn't your fault, Hailey.'

'I know.'

Callum came round the coffee-table and sat down on the edge, facing her. 'Do you? Really?'

She looked into his grey eyes, so close now. His knees were centimetres from hers. 'Yes, really. On an intellectual level, yes.'

'And on an emotional level?'

Hailey sighed. Boy, did he know how to ask the right questions. 'Emotionally, things aren't so clear cut.'

Callum nodded and took another swig of his beer. 'Ain't that the truth.'

Hailey looked at him sharply. 'You blame yourself for Tom?'

'No.' Callum gave a decisive shake of his head. 'I was onto that very quickly.'

Then that only left… 'Annie?'

Callum looked away from her probing gaze. He rolled the beer bottle against his forehead. 'You're not going to tell me not to blame myself? That there was nothing I could have done?'

'I think you know that,' she said gently.

He glared at her. 'I'm a doctor, damn it. I save

people's lives. That's what I do. And yet I couldn't even help my own wife.'

'I know.'

'She wouldn't let me help her. She was so determined to do it herself.'

'I know,' Hailey murmured again, because there wasn't anything else she could say.

Callum rubbed his hand over his hair. 'Annie's parents blame me.'

'Oh, Callum, I don't think—'

'They do. They don't say it but I know they feel that way. I know they think I should have been onto it sooner.'

Hailey nodded, the denial dying on her lips. Paul had never said it either but she had known. 'They need someone to be mad at.'

'Yes.' Callum threw his head back and finished the beer in a few deep swallows. He looked at her and smiled. 'Fine couple we make.'

She gave a half-laugh. 'Yes.' The smiled faded. He was looking at her intensely, his gaze on her mouth. Her pulse stuttered to a halt for a brief second before resuming in triple time. Their moment on the balcony seemed an age ago now but when he looked at her like that, it was as if it had been yesterday.

She picked up his empty beer bottle, pleased to be doing something, breaking the eye contact. She headed into the kitchen, desperate for space. She discarded the empty in the bin under the sink and almost jumped when she realised he'd followed her.

Callum stood in the doorway, suddenly clear about why he'd come tonight. He wanted her. He had since the ball and he didn't want to pretend he didn't any more. 'I want to make love to you.'

Hailey's pulse roared in her head as his husky words stroked across her abdomen like trailing fingers. She held on tight to the bench, not trusting herself when her head was saying *no* but her body was saying *game on*.

She wanted to make love to him too. In fact, she couldn't remember a time when she'd ever wanted something so much. But without analysing them too deeply, she knew her feelings ran much deeper than sex, and she wasn't sure she could play with that kind of fire. She was still sporting scars from the last time. And Callum was vulnerable tonight. After what had happened yesterday, they both were.

Not a good idea.

Hailey swallowed. 'No, you don't. Tom is away and you had a dream about Annie and you don't want to be alone tonight.'

Callum pushed away from the doorframe and walked towards her. 'No, you're wrong. This is nothing to do with Annie or Tom and everything to do with the attraction that we've been ignoring too long. I know we said we shouldn't do this but I can't pretend any more. I see you at work and I want you. I see you in the lift here or lying by the pool and I want you. Even yesterday, when you gave me such a fright, I wanted you. I can't deny it any more.'

Hailey closed her eyes, shutting out his progress towards her, willing him back. Back to the doorway. To the lounge room. To the other side of her front door. To his house. To Melbourne.

'Hailey.'

His voice was near and she opened her eyes to find him standing before her. He was so far up, towering over her.

She wished the distance was greater but at the same time her fingers tingled to pull him closer.

'Callum.'

He heard the note of pleading in her voice. But was it beseeching him to stop or was it asking him not to? 'You know you want this,' he said huskily, gently cupping the side of her face in his hand, tracing his thumb over the contour of her bottom lip.

Hailey sighed, turning her face into his palm. She inhaled his smell and dropped a kiss there. She looked at him. 'We're not teenagers, Callum. Sometimes what we want isn't good for us, sometimes—'

Callum swooped his head down, cutting her off with his mouth. He felt her shock in the momentary paralysis of her lips before a moan escaped from the back of her throat and she relaxed against him, her mouth moving on his.

'Sometimes,' he murmured, pulling away slightly, her lips moist from his, 'it is.'

'But—'

He placed a finger across her lips, his forehead resting against hers. 'Nothing's felt this right in a long time, Hailey.'

She shivered at the catch in his voice, the stroke of his finger against her mouth, the proximity of his lips still only millimetres from hers.

'I know you feel it too,' he murmured.

The intensity of his gaze focusing on her mouth was captivating.

'I think I'm falling for you,' he whispered. He removed his finger and brushed his lips across hers. 'I think I'm falling bad.'

Hailey could barely breathe. His words were mesmerising, his mouth entrancing, his nearness intoxicating. 'Callum,' she croaked.

He kissed her then. Properly. His hands cradled her face and he opened her mouth with the sheer force of his own. His pulse tripped and his breath came in tortured gasps. Hers sounded just as rough, just as wild, and he revelled in her tenuous control as she moaned deep in the back of her throat and yanked him closer by his lapels.

He didn't know what was going to happen after this. What the morning would hold or any of the days after. All he knew was now. Holding her, kissing her, making love with her. This had been their destiny since that very chaste kiss on the balcony. And nothing else mattered.

He straightened, pulling her up with him, lifting her off the floor, grasping her bottom and placing her up on the kitchen bench without pausing for breath. Now they were face to face. He parted her legs, pushing himself between them, planting himself firmly at the juncture of her thighs, her knees cradling his hips.

He broke away, his breath almost painful in his chest. 'You're beautiful,' he said, stroking her hair back from her face, touching her lips, which were swollen from his ministrations.

Hailey ran her tongue along the pads of his fingers. 'So are you.' And she reached for him, pulling his head down, her lips seeking the heat of his, the feel of his, the taste of his. He tasted like beer and man and she moaned at the richness of it.

She felt his hands tighten on her buttocks and he slid her forward, forcing her thighs wider, causing her to lock her legs around his hips. The rough cotton of his clothes, the bulk of his zip and what lay beneath it pressed against her centre and she clung to him as he rubbed against her.

Her breasts were squashed against his chest. The heat between her legs where his erection taunted her was unbearable. She wondered if it was possible to enmesh herself with him, truly become one, through sheer force of will. She felt hot, burning up all over, and still, like a moth, she wanted to be closer to his burning white flame.

She slid her hands down his back, her hands finding his buttocks. They felt round and firm in her grasp and she squeezed, bringing him closer still. He thrust against her and it was sweet, erotic torture.

Her hands crept under his shirt and roamed the contours of his back. His skin was hot and very, very male, and she wanted to see his chest again. To explore it with no fear of interruption. To press her own nakedness against his, feel his heat on her breasts.

She pulled away, her breathing ragged. 'I want to see you,' she told him, her fingers fumbling with his buttons.

Callum groaned as her nails grazed his chest. He claimed her mouth again, plundering her sweetness. Her fingers brushed his stomach and he wanted to tear his shirt off. His lips grew bolder, wanting to have more of her. They devoured the arch of her neck, licking the pulse that beat frantically at the base. They nibbled along the length of her shoulder, moving the singlet strap out of the way with his teeth.

Hailey gave a frustrated growl as the last button eluded her. Callum gnawed at her neck and she pulled at the two sides of his shirt abruptly, ripping them apart. The button popped. She vaguely heard the noise of it landing on the tiles somewhere behind them.

She gave him a triumphant grin and pushed his shirt off

his shoulders and down his arms. It was better than she remembered. Smoother, browner, wider. More sculpted, more defined. She pressed a kiss to the smooth, flat perfection of a pectoral muscle and felt the skin twitch under her lips.

She placed her hand where her mouth had been, her gaze going lower, following the intriguing narrow line of hair that bisected his abs and trailed behind the waistband of his jeans. She let her hand follow the journey her eyes had just taken, coming to rest at the button keeping the rest of him from her.

She glanced up at him.

'Oh, no.' Callum grinned. 'Your turn.' He removed her hand from his waistband and raised her arms above her head, holding her wrists together while he kissed her hard on the mouth. He trailed his fingers down her forearms, down her triceps, grazed the sensitive flesh of her underarm, brushed the swell of her breasts and down her rib cage to where her singlet rested against her stomach.

He pulled away from the kiss and smiled at her as he grasped the hem of her shirt and whisked it up and completely off in seconds.

'Hailey,' Callum breathed, looking his fill, still manacling her wrists above her head.

He brought her arms down slowly, watching her breasts, fascinated by their fullness and the dusky pink of their upturned nipples. He placed her hands, palms down, on the counter behind her, his fingers interlinked with hers, holding them there, making her chest thrust slightly.

'Oh, my.' Callum breathed out again and lowered his head, first kissing one rapidly puckering nipple and then the other.

'Callum.'

He smiled against her chest as he heard the squeak of frustration and she squirmed a little on the bench. He glanced up at her from his position. 'Shh.' Then he turned his attention to a very enticing nipple and opened his mouth over it.

He groaned in satisfaction as she cried out and arched her back. He released her hands and immediately felt them in his hair, caressing it, urging his head closer. He obliged, switching sides, sweeping his arm behind her, bringing her closer, higher, further into his mouth.

Hailey squirmed, wanting to touch all of him, wanting to have him touch all of her. She kicked her feet against the cupboard doors in frustration.

Callum broke away, drunk with lust, his breath harsh with desire. 'Let's get horizontal,' he suggested, sweeping her forward, lifting her bottom off the bench, gratified when her legs tightened around his hips, rubbing intimately against him. She clung to his neck and he almost fell over when she kissed him, squashing her breasts against him, distracting him from his goal, ruining his sense of direction.

They got as far as the nearest kitchen wall before he stopped, pushed her hard against it and returned her kiss. How they made it to her room, he'd never know. Between several wall stops, half-grunted directions and a hand finding its way below his waistband, it was amazing he didn't injure both of them.

They collapsed on her bed. They didn't notice the television still flickering or the multitude of hard, pointy objects barely covered by the thrown-back duvet. They were down and then they were naked, hastily discarding the rest of their clothes, and then they were all over each other. Exploring, touching, learning each other's bodies, discovering their rhythm.

Hailey was no longer earthbound. There was just Callum and herself in a bubble, floating somewhere in space, no need for earthly restrictions. Sensations swirled around her like psychedelic starbursts. Energy and heat and light danced along her nerve endings and fizzed like champagne in her veins.

From the feel of his mouth on her flesh to the eroticism of his hair grazing her stomach to the way he fitted inside her like he was the key that had been made especially for her—it was perfect in every way. There was none of the awkwardness typical of first times. No shyness. No reserve. Just two people finding an ancient rhythm composed especially for them.

When the crescendo came it surpassed all her expectations. He called her name and they rose and fell together, holding each other tight, riding the ripples, spinning and spinning.

Spinning as one. Floating as one. Landing as one—gently, gently, locked together in blissful lassitude. Callum shifted, pulled her into him, spooning her, kissing her neck, whispering sweet nothings as sleep claimed them both.

Callum's last thought was momentous. *I'm not falling. I've fallen.* His arm tightened around her as he felt sleep tug him further under.

He was in love with Hailey Winters.

CHAPTER NINE

CALLUM woke about five the next morning in exactly the same position, the top of Hailey's head tucked under his chin. The first creep of dawn was pushing itself through the gap where the curtains didn't quite meet and his arm had fallen asleep.

Neither of them had moved. Hailey's neck was close and he nuzzled it, inhaling her aroma, dropping a kiss there as he slowly retrieved his arm. She murmured and rolled on her stomach, the sheet slipping to reveal the blemish-free olive perfection of her back and the cheeky rise of her bottom.

He clenched and unclenched his fist, grimacing as the blood returned and a thousand hot pins needled his skin. He ignored them, determined nothing could ruin the sight before him as he allowed his gaze to linger on Hailey's naked form.

Normally, if Tom had sneaked into bed with him in the middle of the night, he woke to his son's foot in his face or orchie in his ribs. At the very least he was woken at the crack of dawn by Tom's excited voice, shaking and begging him to get up, get up.

To be able to lie here and leisurely wake up next to the woman he loved, the gorgeous, naked woman he loved, was extremely gratifying. He'd forgotten how special that could be and he wanted to do it every morning. Yes, they had some issues to resolve but it had taken years to fall in love again and now he had, he didn't want to waste time being apart.

He trailed a finger down her spine and smiled as she murmured again. Her skin was warm and supple and he felt goosebumps against the pads of his fingers. It had been a long time since he'd felt this content, that things were going to work out OK. After six years maybe it was his time to be happy?

When he thought about it, he'd known since the beginning. Just like with Annie. It hadn't just been the moonlight that night or the way she'd been with Tom. There'd been a...flicker...a gut feeling that she was more than sparkly legs and a pretty face. She had intrigued him, bewitched him that night and now he knew why. Because he'd fallen for her. From the second she'd taken Tom's hand, prepared to protect a little boy she didn't know from Adam, he had been an absolute goner.

He rolled on his stomach, his side pressed against hers, and propped himself up on his elbows. He dropped a kiss on her upper arm and another on her shoulder blade. Did she feel the same? She hadn't said anything when he had told her he was falling for her. No *I think I am too* or even *That's great, let me think about it.*

Saturday had freaked her out. Hell, it had freaked him out too. He had withdrawn from her, shut her out, caught up in the heart-pounding fear that something had happened to Tom. But loving her meant loving every part of her. Even the panic merchant. It meant warts and all.

Hailey had baggage that would impact on their lives. He

knew that. But, then, so did he. And he would spend the rest of his life being there for her when the events of her past overwhelmed her, reassuring her. And if she was hyper-vigilant with Tom then so be it. It would be nice to have someone else to share his vigilance with as well as his fears for Tom's future.

Still, he had the feeling she'd be skittish, especially after the events of Saturday. And what if she didn't love him? Just because he had an inkling that she shared his feelings, it didn't mean that she did. She was definitely attracted to him, had admitted it in word and deed. But he wanted more than a physical thing, more than sex.

He wanted what he'd had with Annie. A deep and abiding commitment to each other. A wedding ring. Maybe more children—that little brother for Tom. Despite the tragic end to his marriage, he would never not have done it and he was sure he and Annie would have been together for ever had fate not dealt them a rotten hand. Some of the happiest years of his life had been in his marriage and he was a firm believer in the institution.

He certainly wanted another shot at it. With Hailey.

'Why are you watching me?'

Callum smiled against her shoulder, nuzzling his face into the roundness of it. 'Because I can't believe how lucky I am,' he murmured, his voice muffled as he scattered kisses on her skin.

Hailey smiled and gave a languorous stretch. 'Good answer. What time is it?' she asked, rolling on her back, turning her head to look at the clock.

Callum feasted his eyes on the view that just got even better. His body acted predictably and he felt his pulse rate pick up in anticipation.

'Ugh! Five a.m.?' She turned back to face him. 'What a perfectly indecent hour.'

Good. It matched his perfectly indecent thoughts.

Hailey caught him ogling and felt her nipples grow hard beneath his very sexual gaze. There was no awkward morning-after moment—she felt like she'd been waking up next to him for ever. She was tempted to stretch a bit more, tease him a little. 'You didn't hear what I said, did you?'

He pulled his gaze away from her breasts and grinned. 'You spoke?'

Hailey's toes curled at the streak of pure naughtiness in his voice. She raised herself on her bent elbows thrilled by the way Callum's gaze was glued to her every movement. 'Why are you so far away?' she murmured.

'Good question.' He grinned again and pulled her over on top of him.

Hailey was happy as she cradled her cup of tea in her lap out on the deck with Callum a couple of hours later. It was a glorious Monday morning, the sky was cloudless and the sun sparkled on the Brisbane River below.

Callum was munching on toast, dressed in just his jeans from last night, sitting opposite her, grinning like the cat that had swallowed the cream. She was sitting wrapped in her bathrobe, her combed, wet hair drying in the sun, her face turned towards the still mild rays, her eyes shut. Her feet were propped on his lap. They'd just showered together and she was reliving every sexy detail.

'You know those lapels gape and I can see a good amount of your chest?' Callum mused.

Hailey opened her eyes and looked directly at him. 'Yep.'

Callum laughed. 'Tease.'

She laughed and shut her eyes again. Callum was massaging her feet and she felt like a big old tabby cat, warmed by the sun, stroked by its owner, content and very, very happy.

'Well, I'd love to play hookey for the day like some, but I have to go to work and I need to go home for a change of clothes.' Callum removed her feet reluctantly.

Hailey opened her eyes and sighed. It had been a perfect twelve hours and she didn't want it to end. She'd deliberately not thought about what happened next. She didn't want to have to go back to reality so soon.

'You could just wear that,' she suggested, lifting a foot and tracing her toe down the centre of his stomach, drawing it lightly across his fly area, grinning when he blasted her with a sultry look and grabbed hold of her foot so she couldn't create any more havoc.

He stood, upsetting her position, picking up his mug and plate. 'I'm feeling objectified.'

'Yeah, I know how you guys hate that.'

Callum laughed and skirted her chair, evading her hands. 'I'm going to be late.'

Hailey sighed and gathered her dishes, following Callum inside. 'Here, give them to me,' she said. 'Go get your stuff together.'

Callum passed over his crockery, kissing her hard and brief on the mouth as he did so. She opened her eyes, dizzy from the surge of desire licking at her body, and found him looking at her.

'I like it when you look like that.'

'Like what?' she asked breathily.

Thoroughly kissed. Glazed. Maybe even, *in love*? 'Starry-eyed.' He grinned.

She was about to protest his description, not liking

how…how…teenage-girl-with-a-crush it sounded but, then, she had been staring at him stupidly and grinning at him since five a.m. And as she'd been studiously avoiding calling it—what had happened between them—anything, a crush sounded pretty damn good.

A knock interrupted their conversation and Hailey stared at the door, trying to fathom what to do about it, while her hormones were still directing impulses away from her brain.

Callum laughed. 'Take the dishes.' He kissed her and then turned her round to face the kitchen. 'Snap out of it.' He gave her a gentle push. 'I'll get the door.'

Hailey walked automatically, one foot in front of the other. How did he expect her to snap out of it when he kept kissing her all the time? She got to the sink and looked at the dishes in her hands. What had he said she was to do?

Callum was smiling as he opened the door. It was one of *those* moments. The moment when your life was perfect and you had absolutely no idea that just around the corner, or on the other side of a door, things were about to come crashing to a halt. He'd lived through two of those already and had no reason to doubt that, having been dealt his fair share, he was in line for another.

'Er…oh!'

Callum blinked at the nonplussed-looking man standing on Hailey's doorstep. He didn't have to enquire who it was. It was the man from the photo. Paul.

'I'm terribly sorry. I'm not sure I have the right address. I'm looking for Hailey Winters.'

Callum nodded, the clipped English accent bothering him more than it should have. 'No. No, you have the right address.'

They stared at each other for a moment or two, trying to get the other's measure. Callum could see Paul was confused to be met by a man. A half-naked man at that. He felt his hackles rise. Had he thought she was going to pine away for someone who'd driven her away?

'Do you think I could…come in? Maybe see her?'

Callum detected the faint note of impatience, maybe even arrogance. He wanted to like this man—heaven knew, he felt sorry for him. He could certainly relate to him. He could have been him, after all. *There but for the grace of God and all that.* But at the moment all Paul was was a fly in his ointment.

'Of course.' Callum gave himself a shake and stood aside to admit…who? His rival? The man who Hailey had loved and lost? He noted the sizeable suitcase by Paul's side and felt a creep of alarm. 'I'll just go and…see what she's up to.'

Callum walked to the kitchen, his brain grappling with the implications of Paul's appearance. Hailey was standing at the sink, her back to him. 'Hailey,' he called.

Hailey turned, grateful for the distraction. The water was running and the dishes were in the sink but she was just staring at them, smiling goofily at the rainbows in the bubbles. 'Hmm?'

'You have a…visitor.'

Hailey frowned. At seven-thirty in the morning? The look on Callum's face brought her quickly out of her daydream. She wiped her hand on a teatowel and covered the distance to the doorway quickly. Something was wrong.

She looked up to see Paul standing in the middle of her lounge room. 'Paul?'

Callum shut his eyes at the strange note in her voice. There was surprise, incredulity and something else, something harder to hear. Joy. One word yet full of so much…hope.

Hailey crossed the room in seconds. She threw herself into Paul's arms, amazed to see him, grateful beyond words that he was there. His arms pulled her close and she almost cried it felt so good be held without reserve. Without censure.

She pulled back slightly, so happy to see him she accepted his quick kiss on her mouth without any thought. In fact, she gave him one back. And then kissed each cheek before pulling him back for another long, lingering hug.

Callum clenched his fists, the urge to rip them apart overwhelming. He wanted to break things. He understood that this reunion was always going to be an emotional one but this was on a whole other level. She was in her bathrobe, for crying out loud. She was naked underneath. He'd just been ogling her breasts. Paul had missed his chance. He didn't get to hold her so intimately.

They pulled apart and shared a look so private that Callum despaired about their future.

'Oh, my God, I can't believe you're here,' she whispered.

'Maybe I should have called first?'

Hailey frowned up at him and then turned when Paul indicated behind them. Callum was still standing in the doorway to the kitchen, his chest bare, his eyes shuttered, his jaw rigid.

He was tense. She could see that. But it was too much. All too much to take in. She'd hoped for this moment for a long time, for Paul to come to her, to absolve her, and now it was here, it had to take precedence. She couldn't think about Callum and what had just happened. There was unresolved stuff between her and Paul, closure to be had.

Paul had lost a child, a son the same age as Tom, he needed her more. Surely Callum would understand that?

'Oh, no, Callum was just leaving,' she assured Paul quickly.

Callum felt as if she'd punched him in the solar plexus. This couldn't be happening. She'd just dismissed him as if they were casual acquaintances. Mere friends. Last night they'd been as far removed from friends as possible. Five minutes ago she'd been teasing him with glimpses of her flesh and now another man was touching her. Touching her with familiarity. With a casual ease that spoke of greater intimacy.

She wanted him to go, he could see that. Her eyes were pleading silently with him and he battled with himself to do her bidding, to realise what this meant to her. He forced himself to, his gaze firmly fixed on Paul's hand at her waist. 'Yes. I'll be out of your hair in a moment.'

Callum stalked out of the room and Hailey nearly sagged against Paul in relief. She didn't have time for a macho male showdown, for ego. This was big. This thing that had just happened was big. Bigger, right now, than her and Callum's night of carnal pleasure.

There was so much she wanted to ask Paul, to catch up with. So much was unresolved. She wanted to know how he was. How he'd been doing. Paul and Eric had been such a big part of her life and there was no denying she'd left a part of her heart behind in London.

When Callum came back into the lounge fully dressed he discovered Paul and Hailey on the lounge, talking quietly, sitting close, their knees almost touching, her still in her bathrobe. He clenched his fist around his keys, wanting to drag her away, to demand she get dressed, order her to stand by his side.

They looked up as he entered the room. 'I'll ring you tonight,' he said.

Hailey saw the stormy conflict in his gaze, the whites of his knuckles. She stood and moved until she was standing in front of him. 'Thank you,' she mouthed. She wanted to reach up and touch his jaw, place her hands on his chest, but felt too awkward in the circumstances.

'We need to talk,' he murmured.

She nodded. 'Not now. Soon.'

Callum looked into her deep brown eyes. He saw the pitch and roll of emotion as she grappled with the situation. He saw her sincerity but also saw her struggle. 'I'll call tonight.'

He lowered his head to kiss her. Whatever the hell had just happened in the last fifteen minutes, it didn't seem right not to. He'd fallen in love last night and he wasn't going to pretend that hadn't happened or he hadn't kissed every inch of her body because her old boyfriend was back in town.

Hailey averted her face and his lips fell chastely on her cheek. Like the first time. Except nothing had ever been chaste between them. Even that first time there had been an undercurrent, a foretelling of the future. She could sense his disappointment, his disapproval, and she squeezed his arm, begging him to understand.

Callum bade Paul a curt goodbye and left. So not how he'd pictured that this morning would go. So not the way he'd wanted them to part.

Having the day with Paul was cathartic for Hailey, to say the least. They talked a lot about Eric and that day and the days that had followed. And about them and their break-up and Donna. He told her about his new job and rebuild-ing his life. He also made no secret of the fact that he wanted her to be part of it. That he'd forgiven her, absolved her and was ready to love her.

Which was what she'd wanted all along. To hear him say those words. At the time she'd have stayed without hesitation, been part of his life, and helped him through the dark times. She'd begged him to. Pleaded with him to allow her to take care of him, despite how he had betrayed her with his ex. But he'd sent her away.

And she'd understood that. He had been a father who had just lost a son. He hadn't been capable of worrying about anyone else's feelings or needs. So she'd comforted herself with the fact that he was grieving and she'd left, come back to Australia to lick her wounds and hope that he would come for her some day.

And so now he was here, telling her all the things she had wanted to hear back then. So, what was the problem? This was what she'd wanted, wasn't it? But things weren't as clear cut as they had been back then. A lot of water had flowed under the bridge and she was a much stronger person.

Her confidence as a nurse, which had taken a massive battering, was slowly returning. Her days that had had no direction other than survival had purpose and structure, and a man had come into her life wanting her, accepting her.

She could see her reticence confused Paul. He'd obviously thought she was just going to say all was forgotten and fall back into his arms. And if she was honest with herself, she'd admit his assumption rankled. Yes, he'd been hurt, he'd been grieving, but, then, so had she.

He had discarded her. Trampled all over her love.

Finding him in bed with his ex had cut her so deeply that she'd doubted she could ever love again. Did he expect her to just wipe that under the carpet?

Callum checked his mobile message bank all day. He hoped desperately one of the messages that were flashing on his machine when he got home in the evening would be from her. One was from Tom. Two were from his secretary. And one was a hang-up. He lasted an hour before he dialled her number.

'Hi, this is Hailey's voicemail, I'm busy right now so leave a message.'

Busy? Busy doing what? Callum's heart thudded in his chest while he waited for the beep. He thought of several things to say and discarded them all. He'd give anything to hear her voice. Her real voice. To be with her, lying beside her as he had done last night. Why did it seem such an age ago now?

He replaced the phone as several scenarios of what she was doing right now popped into his head.

Stop it!

The apartment was quiet and he found himself wishing Tom was there. At least there was never a silent moment or time to indulge in his own thoughts with an energetic six-year-old around. At least Tom kept his mind off things and caring for his son took up all his energy. There was usually nothing left of him at the end of the day and right now it seemed exceedingly inviting.

He channel-surfed for a while, glancing at the wall clock every couple of minutes. It hit seven-thirty and the evening alone with his thoughts stretched interminably ahead. He stood. He couldn't do it. He couldn't wait around. He had to know. Callum was at her door in under a minute, banging loud enough to announce his presence to the entire floor.

Hailey hurried to the door—had Paul lost the key? She blinked at Callum's glowering presence. His shirt was untucked and dark stubble shadowed his jaw. He obviously hadn't shaved after he'd left that morning. He looked big and mad and handsome and she realised after an exhausting day of reflection and analysis with Paul how much she'd missed him. 'Hi.'

Callum stood on the doorstep, his eyes greedily roving over her face and body, her presence momentarily striking him dumb. It was a few moments before he recovered. 'We need to talk.'

'Callum.' Hailey shut her eyes. It was so good to see him, to hear his voice. Had it only been last night they'd made love?

'Can I come in?'

She sighed. 'Callum.'

'Please?'

His voice was husky and full of yearning and she wanted to do more than just invite him in. She wanted to take him into her bed, put her head on his shoulder and listen to the steady thud of his heart. She stood aside.

Callum braced himself to be polite to Paul as he brushed past her and stepped into her apartment. 'Where's Paul?' he asked, looking around the empty lounge room.

'He's gone to the bottle shop,' Hailey murmured, skirting Callum to stand nervously beside the lounge.

How cosy. 'So, what's been happening today?'

'We've talked. A lot. It's been…cathartic.'

Callum frowned. He heard the weariness in her voice. 'He hasn't been upsetting you has he?'

'No. Of course not.'

'So where does this leave us?'

'Callum, please. I need some closure. I need this time with Paul, please…'

Callum clenched his fists. 'So was I just a substitute lover? Until the real thing came back into your life?'

Hailey reached for the lounge as she staggered from his insult. 'It wasn't like that, and you know it. What happened between you and I was…' Hailey sighed wearily. She'd talked so much today her voice hurt.

'Was?' he demanded.

'Something I can't think about right now. How was I to know that he was going to show up on my doorstep?'

'Isn't that what you'd been hoping for?'

Today had been a day for honesty and Hailey didn't see the point in stopping now. 'Yes. Deep down, yes. In the beginning I did hope he would,' she admitted. 'But I never expected it.'

Callum felt her slipping away. 'So you've always been holding out a little for him?'

'No. Yes… I don't know. All I know is that my life changed irrevocably over a year ago—'

'And it didn't change irrevocably on Sunday night?'

Hailey shut her eyes. Of course it had. 'You know what I mean, Callum. Paul dumping me, Eric's death…it tore my life to pieces and only Paul can help me put it back together.'

'No, you're wrong, Hailey.'

Hailey felt a lump rise in her throat. 'You don't understand,' she said, choking on a sob.

'I don't understand?' Callum growled, ignoring the anguish evident in her voice. He closed the distance between them and reached for her. 'I don't understand? Let me tell you, Hailey, I know about pieces. Little tiny pieces of your life that are torn from you and shredded and strewn everywhere and there's nothing you can do about it and nothing's the same ever again and you have to go on even though you're bleeding and injured and all you want to do is curl up and die. I know about irrevocable changes. Trust me on this. I. Can. Help. You.'

A tear escaped and trekked down her cheek. Poor Callum, how much he had suffered. But this was about her survival, her closure. She knew what she needed for that. For the first time, thanks to him, she knew.

'No, Callum. I need to do this. I need to see this through to the end. Alone.'

Callum shook his head and released her. How had he picked another woman who was so hell bent on rejecting his help? 'God, what is it with women? You're just like Annie.'

'No Callum. I'm not. I'm nothing like Annie. I didn't stay and fight tooth and nail like she did. I wasn't strong like she was. I fell apart. I left with my tail between my legs. I ran away. But not any more. I have to face this now. I can't run from it any more.'

'But she never let me help her either.'

Hailey heard the anguish in his voice and her heart went out to him. She lifted her hand to his cheek. 'Because Annie knew something I've only just realised. Some things you just have to do on your own.' She dropped her hand. 'Just give me this time with him. Please, Callum. If you feel anything for me at all, you'll let me do this my way.'

Callum ran his hand through his hair. *If he felt anything for her?* Damn it, he loved her! It killed him to think he couldn't help her.

He sighed. 'OK.'

Hailey shut her eyes briefly. She reached for his hand and was grateful he didn't reject the gesture. She gazed down at their interlocked fingers. 'Thank you, Callum.'

He squeezed her hand. 'I'll see you at work? When are you back on?'

'Day after tomorrow,' she murmured.

He gave her hand another squeeze before dropping it. 'The day after tomorrow, then.'

'Sure.'

CHAPTER TEN

HAILEY'S STOMACH fluttered uneasily, feeling like a herd of elephant butterflies had taken up residence when she returned to work. She knew she'd see Callum at some stage today. Hell, she'd be lying if she didn't admit that a large part of her was looking forward to it. But mostly she felt nervous. She knew he wanted answers. But the truth was she didn't have any—just more questions. It should have been clear cut but it wasn't.

The day was busy, for which she was grateful. No time to glance at the swing door every time it opened. No time to worry about who was on the other end of the constantly ringing phone. No time to wonder why he hadn't appeared yet or speculate about to when he would.

Morning tea came and went, so did lunch. Home time was only an hour away and Hailey couldn't figure out if she was relieved or annoyed. Was he trying to punish her, give her a dose of her own medicine? Or had he just got caught up with his private patients or down in Emergency? They'd already had several admissions from them that day as it was.

Soon though, Callum's presence, or lack of it, quickly faded as Hailey became worried about the two-month-old that had been admitted a couple of hours ago. The little girl,

Sarah, had come up via Emergency for investigation of a febrile illness, query viral in origin. She had a two-day history of lethargy, poor feeding and vomiting. All the usual tests had been run in Emergency—blood and urine—and she had a peripheral drip running. Prophylactic antibiotics had been commenced until the cause of the infection had been isolated.

In the two hours she'd been on the ward she'd been stable but her condition in the last ten minutes had worsened. Her fever had just spiked to forty-one and her extremities were now mottled, with very poor perfusion. Worst of all she was becoming less and less responsive.

Rosemary smiled at her as she ducked into the bay, looking for one of the ward's tympanic thermometers. 'Do you know where Yvonne is?' Hailey asked.

'She was in her office a minute ago,' Rosemary said.

'Can you, please, get her for me?' Hailey asked, trying to keep the feeling of dread from rising in her chest and escaping in her voice.

Still, she must have looked pretty serious because Rosemary left immediately, returning with Yvonne.

'What's wrong?' Yvonne asked, cutting to the chase.

Hailey breathed a sigh of relief. 'I don't like the look of her.' She rattled off her concerns to Yvonne. 'Can you page the reg, please?'

Yvonne left immediately and Hailey placed some flow by oxygen near the baby's face. She noted that Sarah's pulse displayed on the saturation monitor seemed to have plateaued at about one hundred and ninety. The fever was no doubt responsible for some of the alarming figure, but she checked it herself to make sure it was right. The brachial pulse bounded beneath her touch so rapidly it was hard to count. In fact, Sarah's entire abdomen pulsed with the pounding of her heart.

'Do you know where her mum went?' Hailey asked Rosemary.

'She said she was going home to sort out the other kids. She said she'd only be an hour.'

'OK, thanks.' Hailey nodded as she hit the button to take another blood pressure measurement and checked the baby's pupils while she waited. Still briskly reactive but Sarah wasn't responding to any of Hailey's interventions.

Callum entered 2B quickly. Yvonne had left him in no doubt that it was urgent and he hadn't wasted any time getting here. He strode to the bay, faltering when he saw Hailey at the bedside. He'd known it was her first shift back, had been trying his damnedest to get here all day, but things had been crazy and everything had conspired against him. And one look at the baby told him now wasn't the time for chatting.

'What have we got?'

Hailey looked up from her tiny patient, startled to find Callum here. She'd been expecting his registrar, Adele Nolan, who was an excellent doctor, more than capable of handling the situation.

Anyway, it didn't matter. Not even this moment that she'd been dreading and anticipating all day mattered. Seeing him again after their tête-à-tête the other night was strange, and she felt her pulse leap at his sheer masculinity, but she paid it no heed. There was enough adrenaline charging around her system at the moment to kick-start a generator. And all their issues had to take a back seat to the grimness of Sarah's situation.

Hailey filled Callum in on her recent deterioration as if they'd been doing this together for ever. 'I think she's septic.'

Callum nodded, his concern for the very unwell-looking baby also overriding the million things he wanted to say to Hailey. 'BP?' he asked as he took his stethoscope out and listened to the baby's chest.

'Fifty-five systolic.'

He nodded, listening over the entire lung field. He palpated the abdomen. 'Let's give her some extra fluid. What's her access like?'

'Good cubital fossa,' Hailey said, indicating the drip at the crook of the baby's elbow.

'Twenty per kilo. Let's fill her up and get her to ICU.'

Hailey and Callum worked on reversing the shocked infant while Yvonne did some ringing around. First she rang ICU to organise a consult and a bed and then she rang Sarah's mother on her mobile to tell her to come back to the hospital immediately.

The ICU team arrived, consisting of a nurse and a doctor, and they all worked together to stabilise the baby. Twenty minutes later Sarah was intubated and hooked up to a portable ventilator and monitor. The extra fluid had also gone in and her heart rate and blood pressure had both improved slightly.

'We'll get a central line and an arterial line in when we get back to the unit,' Glenda Collins, the ICU doctor, told Callum. 'We might need to start some inotropes too if the blood pressure remains too saggy. Are we ready to go, Kyle?' she asked the nurse who had accompanied her.

Yvonne paged an orderly and a few minutes later the cot, loaded with portable machines, was wheeled out of the ward, flanked by two wardsmen, Glenda and Kyle. Sarah looked very, very tiny, dwarfed by all the medical personnel and equipment.

Yvonne, Hailey and Callum watched them leave.

'Will she be all right, do you think?' Rosemary asked, standing back in the corridor to allow the cot to pass.

Hailey looked at the junior nurse. 'I hope so.' She smiled. 'Fingers crossed.'

'She has a very good chance,' Callum butted in. 'Thanks to Hailey's quick intervention.'

Hailey blushed at his compliment. She'd handled it well. She knew that. She'd felt calm and confident. Sure, her heart was beating a little fast, but that was only to be expected when a baby's life was on the line. Even the most hardened professionals succumbed to the effects of adrenaline, they just knew how to channel it to their advantage.

A year ago something like this would have really thrown her. But she'd come a long way since then. Callum made her feel like she could do anything.

'Are you OK?' he asked her, his hand on her shoulder.

She smiled at him. 'I'm fine. Thanks for coming so promptly.'

He shrugged. 'Yvonne said it was urgent.'

She nodded. 'Thanks anyway.'

He looked at her, saw the dark smudges under her eyes. 'How are things…?'

Hailey hesitated for a moment. 'OK.'

'Do you need to talk?' She looked like she needed to talk.

Hailey looked at her watch. Her shift was nearly over. It was surprisingly tempting. He looked so good and she had missed him. 'I can come to your office in half an hour?'

Callum gave her shoulder a squeeze. 'Thirty minutes. That would be great.'

Hailey felt more nervous standing in front of Callum's office door than she had when Sarah had gone bradycardic, her heart rate having plummeted right down to forty during intubation. But she'd known why that had happened. She knew about the vagal nerve and how stimulating it could cause a drop in the pulse rate. And she'd known a dose of atropine would fix it.

But there wasn't a drug to fix the twisted triangle she found herself in. Paul wanting her. Callum wanting her. Paul, who had come back into her life like she'd once hoped he would. Paul, who was finally past what had happened with Eric and was prepared to forgive her and move on. Paul, who had betrayed her trust and sent her away.

Callum wanting her. Callum, who she'd been wildly attracted to from the beginning. Callum, whose past was littered with tragedy but who had gone on, refusing to be cowed. Callum, who was still in love with his dead wife.

She summoned her nerve and knocked on the door.

Callum looked up from the computer screen he was feigning interest in. He closed the application with a click of the mouse. 'Come in.'

Hailey entered as Callum was rising from his chair. 'Hi,' she said, shutting the door after her.

'Hi.' They looked at each other for a few moments. He'd missed her. His arms had ached and his heart had felt heavy and he hated how the space beside him in bed that had been empty for six years suddenly seemed so cold. 'Sit,' he said, pulling out a chair for her, remembering his manners.

Hailey sat. She was conscious of him looming over her and she didn't breathe easily until he resumed his seat. He looked tired, his tie, sporting frogs in tiaras, had been loosened, his top button undone.

'So. What's happening with you? You look tired,' he said tentatively.

'So do you.'

'Guess neither of us is getting much sleep.'

Hailey nodded. 'He wants me to go back with him,' she blurted out.

Callum felt his heart stop in his chest before it resumed at a more rapid pace. 'And what do you want?' he asked, breathing carefully, concentrating on staying calm and using logic and reason instead of petty, macho jealousy.

Hailey massaged her forehead. 'I should want it, too.'

'Should?'

'It's what I'd hoped for when I left the UK.' She looked at him beseechingly, trying to make him understand how big this was for her.

'And lately?'

Hailey shook her head and smiled sadly. 'No. Not lately. Lately I'd started to forget…to feel good about my life. About being here.' *About you.* 'But… Oh, heavens, Callum, I didn't think he was ever really going to show up like this. I mean, I'd hoped…back in the beginning but…I'm so confused.'

Callum counted five even breaths. 'Well, I wish I could help you with that, Hailey, but I'm a little confused myself.'

'He says he forgives me. That he doesn't blame me. Do you know how long I've waited to hear that?'

'Forgive you?' Callum frowned. 'What for?'

Hailey looked at him. 'Oh, for Pete's sake, Callum,' she muttered. 'Don't be so bloody obtuse. For Eric, of course.'

Callum felt his hackles rise. 'Well, that's very magnanimous of him.'

He'd tried to cut Paul some slack. He knew intimately how upside down and inside out things could become. But making Hailey feel bad about something that hadn't been her fault was wrong. Letting her continue to beat herself up about it was worse. Making a big deal of absolving her for it was just plain screwed up.

'Hey. His son died, Callum,' she said sharply. 'Eric died.'

Callum rose and leaned over the desk. 'Yes, he did. And that wasn't your fault.'

'I was employed to care for him.' She glared at him.

'Oh, God.' He shook his head and sat down again. 'You do still blame yourself for this.'

The crazy thing was that she didn't, not any more. Or at least she hadn't. But seeing Paul again, reliving all those memories, hearing him talk about forgiveness and absolution, she'd been sucked back into the doubt and insecurities of that time.

'You think going back to England with him, being with him, will absolve you? You want to be part of a couple where you're going to be apportioned the role of blame? Where your place in the relationship rests on your guilt and his sick way of punishing you?'

Hailey shut her eyes and wished she could shut her ears to his criticism. 'Eric was six, Callum. Tom's age.'

'And he contracted meningitis and he died. And it was rapid and virulent and it sucked. It wasn't fair. It was just some random, screwed-up, life's-a-bitch occurrence. Like my wife dying. Like Tom getting leukaemia. Like today, with Sarah. How quickly did her sepsis develop?'

Hailey blinked, her brain sluggishly searching back for the information. 'She deteriorated over about fifteen minutes.'

'Right. So from sick but stable to crashing in a heap in a quarter of an hour. Why's that, do you think?' he fired at her.

'She compensated until she couldn't any more.'

'Right.' He nodded with a satisfied bob of his head.

'Compensation—kids do it really well. I bet Eric's body did it really well too. Just like Sarah.'

'But we got to Sarah in time, didn't we?'

'Sarah was already in hospital. Eric wasn't. He had a very aggressive form of meningitis, Hailey. No one could have saved him.'

'If I'd got him to hospital sooner…'

'No, Hailey. No. There's absolutely nothing to forgive and no blame to apportion. It wasn't your fault and I'll be damned if I'll let him dump this on you.'

Hailey felt tears prick her eyes at Callum's vehement defence of her. She shrugged. 'He was grieving.'

'And what about you, Hailey? Didn't you love Eric too? You sure looked like you did in that photograph.'

She blinked her tears away. 'He was Eric's father, Callum. I think that's a little different.'

'So because you weren't a blood relation, because you didn't give birth to him, your feelings didn't matter? Didn't you need his reassurance, his support?'

'His son had just died. I guess he wasn't thinking about anyone else,' she said wearily.

'Doesn't look like much has changed.'

'Callum,' she said reproachfully.

'He's not a priest, Hailey. And you didn't commit any sins. He can't give you the absolution you seek. No one but you can do that.'

Hailey rubbed her temples. Callum was being less than tolerant of Paul. Surely he of all people should understand? 'Is it so wrong to want to live the rest of my life knowing he doesn't blame me?'

'No, it's just human. But until you stop blaming yourself, is it going to matter what he or anybody else thinks?'

'He says he loves me.'

Callum rubbed his hand over his head, this conversation too, too much for him to comprehend. 'He's got a funny way of showing it.'

'Callum.'

'What? First he drops you like a hot cake when his ex-wife came back on the scene and then it took him over a year to figure things out?'

She ignored his barb about the ex. 'I think he's had a bit on his plate,' she said derisively.

'What happens when his ex comes back again?'

Hailey felt suddenly chilled, thinking about the disruption Donna had caused the first time around. She brushed her hands up and down her arms. 'Donna's remarried,' she said quietly.

He noticed the stiltedness of her voice and realised this tack wasn't getting him anywhere. He sighed. 'Do you love him?' She opened her mouth to answer but he was so afraid she'd say yes he continued, qualifying his question further. 'I mean, truly love him, not out of some sense of guilt or blame or some warped way of apologising for imagined wrongs.'

Callum braced himself for her answer. Had she been holding a candle for Paul the whole time they'd been attracted to each other? What if her guilt led her to make the ultimate sacrifice?

Well, damn it all, he was used to fighting, wasn't he? He'd fought for Annie and for Tom and if she thought he'd stand aside and let her go to Paul out of some weird sense of duty, that he wouldn't fight like hell for her, she was wrong. He had already lost one woman he loved, he wasn't going to sit back and lose another.

She looked at him. 'I don't think I know what love is any more.'

'Yeah? Well, I know what its not. It's not reproachful or condescending or unforgiving. It doesn't hold to ransom or indulge in subtle bribery. It doesn't punish and it's certainly not aloof.'

Hailey's heart thudded in her chest and pounded in her ears. He hadn't taken his eyes off her. 'You seem to know an awful lot about it.'

'Of course I do, Hailey. I'm looking at it. I'm in love with you.' He stood, waiting for her to say something. She stared at him for what seemed an age and he shoved his hands in his pockets. 'I realised the other night, after we'd made love. But I think I knew even before that. Do you remember taking Tom's hand at the ball? Protecting him from my wrath?'

Hailey smiled and nodded, remembering the night Tom had scared the life out of her, drawn to her stockings like a moth to a flame.

'Then. That was the moment.'

'Oh, Callum…'

'No, it's OK. You don't have to say anything. I know you're dealing with a lot at the moment and I don't want some knee-jerk reaction in either direction. But I needed you to know. Wanted you to know.'

Hailey hadn't expected this. She knew there was an attraction between them that she'd never experienced in her life before. Not with any of a string of pretty boys pre-London and certainly not with Paul. But love? She hadn't expected that. She stood. 'I don't know what to say.'

Callum felt a crushing sense of loss and disappointment. *'I love you too' is customary.* 'I think if you don't know the answer then that's pretty telling.'

'No, Callum,' she said hastily. 'This is a lot to take in with everything else… My head is spinning.'

He nodded, jamming his hands further into his pockets. He wanted to take her in his arms and kiss her. Hold her tight until the frown line between her brows vanished and the confusion in her eyes disappeared. 'You should go.'

She took a step towards him. 'Callum—'

He held up his hand. 'It's OK, Hailey. I'm a big boy and you have a lot to think about.'

Hailey nodded absently, and searched in her bag for her keys locating them after a few moments. 'Say hi to Tom for me.'

'I will.'

Callum watched her leave. He sat as the door shut after her. He placed his head on the desk.

That went well.

And think she did. All the way to her apartment, mulling over the things Callum had said. About being a slave to her guilt, being chained by it, unable to move forward. And about his stunning confession.

He loved her? It seemed crazy but she believed him. She'd seen the sincerity oozing from him. He loved her. Since the moment she'd taken Tom's hand.

Paul was waiting for her at the door when she arrived home. 'I missed you today.'

She looked into his face, searching his gaze. She hadn't missed him. She'd thought about Callum and been absorbed in her work and, yes, she'd thought about Paul and him wanting her to go back to the UK. But she hadn't missed him. Not like she'd missed Callum this past two days. There'd been none of the anticipation inside her as she'd driven home to Paul that had been there that morning going to work, knowing she would be seeing Callum.

She smiled at Paul, averting her face so his lips landed somewhere near her ear.

'Everything OK?' Paul frowned.

'Sure,' she dismissed. She headed towards the kitchen, turning back to ask, 'When did you realise you loved me?'

She watched the puzzled look on Paul's face. Eric had looked at her like that when she'd asked him to do something and he had been trying to fathom why.

'A few weeks ago.' He shrugged. 'The counsellor I was telling you about, she was urging me to look around my life, to evaluate it, and it's been so…empty. And we used to have such good times, do you remember, you, me and Eric? And I want that back. I want to laugh again. We always laughed when we were with you.'

Hailey nodded her head slowly. They had laughed a lot. With Eric. In fact, all their happy memories were bundled up with Eric. But looking at Paul now, standing before her, it was obvious that Eric had been their glue. Had she stayed and they'd somehow managed to weather the storm of grief, they would have had nothing keeping them together. 'Yes, we did. We laughed a lot. But that's not love, Paul.'

'We did love each other. Before Donna came back and complicated things. Before Eric…before he…'

'Before Eric died. He died, Paul. You can't even say the word.'

'It's hard, damn it!' Paul yelled.

Hailey's nerves jumped at the reprimand in his voice. She swallowed a lump and felt tears come to her eyes. 'It wasn't my fault.' She looked straight at him.

'Please, Hailey, you don't have to worry about that any more. I've moved on. It happened and I don't want you to beat yourself up about it any longer.'

She'd been waiting for him to agree. To say, yes, he knew it wasn't her fault. But suddenly she realised she was never going to hear it. Callum had been right. She'd let him blame her. Subconsciously allowed him to heap guilt on her. Eric's death had been sudden and tragic. But just as with Sarah's rapid deterioration, it hadn't been her fault.

'It wasn't my fault,' she repeated. 'And I'm not going to beat myself up about it any more.'

'Good.'

She looked at him for a long moment. They'd shared something special for a while that may have grown into something lasting had a hand grenade not been thrown into their happy suburban existence. But all she felt for him now was a residual sense of loss. She couldn't give him what he needed and he certainly couldn't give her what she needed. Unconditional love.

'Sit down, Paul, we need to talk.'

Tom and his grandparents were waiting for him when Callum got home from work and he was grateful for the distraction. Tom's chatter filled up all the aching places in his heart and it felt so good to hold his squirming little body on his lap again.

Callum was relieved, though, when Tom went to bed a couple of hours later without complaint. Tom had been so wound up that Callum had been prepared for him to bounce off the walls until late in the evening, but days of sun and surf had obviously worn him out. He tucked Tom in, brushing the hair off his son's face as he dropped a kiss on his forehead.

'Daddy, when can I see Hailey?'

Callum stilled. Where had that come from? He wished he could say tomorrow. Or, better still, tell Tom to go in and say goodnight to Hailey right now. But he didn't want to promise Tom anything he couldn't deliver. Which was one of the reasons he shouldn't have let himself or his son get too close in the first place. If Hailey rejected his love, took off to England with Paul, he wouldn't be the only one who suffered.

'I'm not sure, Tom.' He smiled. 'I think maybe Hailey needs some time to herself and we need to—'

A pounding at the front door interrupted his careful speech. He looked at his watch. 'Who could that be?' he asked Tom.

'Can I go?' Tom pleaded. Callum looked down into his beseeching gaze. 'OK, but then it's straight to bed,' he agreed, swinging his son up into his arms.

Hailey banged for a second time on Callum's front door. Her heart pounded and her hands shook and she was so nervous she wanted to throw up. But there'd been no thought of putting this off. Waiting till the morning.

Callum was balancing Tom on his shoulders when he opened the door to her. 'Hailey,' Tom shouted enthusiastically, bouncing up and down on his father's shoulders.

To say Callum was stunned to see her was an understatement. He hadn't expected to see or hear from her so soon. She looked awful. Her eyes were red-rimmed, her nose was red, her face was blotchy and she was still in her uniform. 'Hell, are you OK?' he asked as he wrestled Tom off his shoulders.

'Why are you crying, Hailey?' Tom asked.

'Oh, dear, sorry, it's nothing,' Hailey dismissed, sniffling. She must look a state. She'd cried on and off for the last couple of hours. Her talk with Paul had been heart-wrenching and they'd both shed tears. Closing that chapter of her life had been hard, turning her back on Paul when he needed her very difficult. But she couldn't be his emotional scapegoat any longer. And he needed to start his life afresh.

All three of them stood in the doorway, staring at each other. Callum felt a slow rise of dread. She was on his doorstep and had obviously been crying. Was she leaving with Paul? Was that what she'd come to tell him?

'Do you think I could come in?' she asked after a few moments.

'Oh, of course, yes, I'm sorry, come in,' Callum said, standing aside. 'I was just about to put Tom to bed.'

'Yay! Hailey can read me a story!' Tom jumped up and down excitedly.

'Oh, no, Tom, I don't think Hailey—'

'Nonsense,' Hailey interrupted, grinning down at Tom. 'I'd love to. Lead the way, young man.' She held out her hand and let Tom tug her along to his room.

Callum hovered outside the door as Hailey read two books to Tom. He paced a lot as well. What was she doing here? Surely if it had been as the bearer of bad news she wouldn't be wasting time reading to Tom?

'Da-a-ady-y-y.'

That was his cue. He walked into Tom's room and felt his heart flip in his chest at the sight before him. Hailey on her back, her arm around Tom, her shoes off. Tom was snuggled into her side, his faithful torch pressed to her chest. This was what he wanted. For him and for Tom. Every night.

He grinned at his son. 'You yelled?'

'You didn't kiss me goodnight,' Tom said.

'Ah, very remiss of me.'

He leaned down, excruciatingly conscious of the fact his body had to lean over Hailey's to get to Tom's. He could smell her, see her lips in his peripheral vision.

Tom puckered up and Callum laughed as he pressed a brief kiss to Tom's exaggerated lips and then one on his forehead. Tom threw his arms enthusiastically around his father's neck and pulled him down for a great big squeeze, bringing Callum's chest into intimate contact with Hailey's. Callum held his breath, waiting for her to push him away or shrink from his touch.

Hailey shut her eyes as Callum's aftershave enveloped her. She didn't even feel the press of the hard torch into her rib cage so caught up was she in the divine smell of Callum's skin.

Tom released his father and Callum moved away. Hailey didn't want him to pull back. She wanted him to stay close. It had been so intimate and further cemented the feeling that this was where she belonged. 'What about me?'

Callum paused. 'I'm sorry?'

'Don't I get a kiss?'

'Yeah, Daddy, Hailey wants one too.'

Callum's heart pounded. 'Ah...sure?'

Hailey smiled at the confusion in his gaze and nodded at him. His face moved closer to hers and she shut her eyes as his lips descended. And landed on her forehead. She opened them again to protest as he was moving back. 'Hey, how come I only get one?'

'Hailey...' It really wasn't fair for her to tease like this if she was going off to the other side of the world. Unless...

'On the mouth, like Tom,' she said, looking at him innocently and puckering up.

'Hailey.'

She heard the strangled warning note in his voice and blinked up at him with mock coyness. She also heard his sigh but didn't dare shut her eyes this time. When his lips touched hers she softened hers and held on tight around his neck so he couldn't drop a quick peck, like he had with Tom.

Callum jerked back, his chest heaving, his eyes trying to read the message in hers. They didn't look like eyes that had bad news to impart. He backed away and grabbed Hailey by the arm, pulling her upright. 'Say goodnight to Hailey, Tom. We have to go talk now.'

Hailey kissed Tom on the forehead, conscious of Callum's hand in hers tugging at her gently, 'Goodnight, Tom. Don't let the bedbugs bite.'

'Or get in my ears.' He giggled.

'Especially that.' She laughed back, ruffling his hair.

Hailey had walked two paces out of the room when Callum jerked her into his arms and kissed her full on the mouth. She groaned against his lips, snaking her arms up around his neck and rubbing her hands over his velvety hair.

'Please, tell me this is what I think it is and not your warped way of saying goodbye,' he gasped, pulling away.

She smiled and nodded at him, her finger flattening the frown crinkling his forehead. 'I love you, Callum. I'm so sorry it took me a while to get it.'

Callum laughed, not quite believing what was happening. 'Well, it was definitely worth the wait.' He swooped his head down to kiss her again.

'No, wait.' She laughed, pressing her fingers to his mouth. 'I think we need to talk a little first.'

'Really?' He pouted, his hands travelling south over the rise of her delectable derrière. 'Can't we do that later?'

'No.' She smiled as she removed his hands from her butt.

They moved into the lounge room. 'What happened?' he asked.

'I got home after talking to you and I realised I didn't love him. Not any more. Not the way he needed me to.'

Callum sat on the lounge, his legs suddenly weak from relief. 'It took you long enough.'

She grinned at him. 'That's why I was so confused, I think. It'd been bugging me why I wasn't falling all over him. He was here and a year ago that had been all that I'd wanted so why wasn't I leaping into his arms? Why was I holding back?'

'And why was that?'

'Because I was in love with you.'

Callum held out his hand and when she took it he pulled her down beside him, snuggling her close, kissing the top of her head. 'Good answer. When did you know?'

Hailey thought back and smiled, locating the exact moment easily. 'That night on the balcony when you were dancing with Tom after midnight.'

She sighed against his chest, rubbing her face into his shirt. 'I think I was coming to the realisation the night we made love and then Paul showed up and everything got so messed up.'

They sat in silence for a few minutes, holding each other. 'Where's Paul now?'

'I drove him to a hotel.'

'How did he take the news?'

Hailey sat up. 'Not well at first. But we had a long talk. He admitted he's always blamed me for Eric's death and could see that it was unfair and he and I would never have worked out. Eric had always been our glue.'

Callum cradled her face with his hands and ran his thumbs gently under her eyes where they'd been all red half an hour ago. 'He upset you?'

Hailey placed a hand over his. 'No. It was just sad, that's all. Cathartic and emotional and…sad to close a chapter of my life that has been so turbulent. But I think he's going to be OK. He confronted some things he'd been hiding from so, yeah, I think it'll work out for him eventually.'

'Are you OK?' he asked gently.

She smiled. 'I am now.'

Callum leaned forward and rained light kisses on her eyes, her nose, her cheeks and her mouth.

'How do you feel about marrying me?' he asked, pulling away from her lips reluctantly.

Hailey looked into his eyes, searching for any uncertainty. 'Are you sure?'

'Of course.' He frowned down at her, sensing her hesitation. 'Why wouldn't I be?'

Hailey took a breath. 'Because of Annie.'

'Annie?'

'I think you might still be in love with her and I'm not her, Callum. I've already been with one man who chose another woman over me and I don't want to invest in this to discover that I'm never going to match up. A real woman I can compete with. I can't compete with a ghost.'

'Oh, no, no, no,' Callum denied quickly, cupping her face in his palms and dropping kisses on her closed eyelids. 'A piece of me is always going to belong to Annie, as I'm sure a piece of you is always going to belong to Paul. She's Tom's mother and I loved her deeply. But I'm not *in love* with Annie. My heart is too full of you. It yearns for you. It adores only you. You are the woman of my dreams. Annie was my past. You are my future.'

Hailey felt a lump in her throat at the poetry of his words. His sincerity and love shone down at her. 'Well, in that case,' she whispered, her voice husky with barely contained tears, 'I'd like very much to marry you.'

Callum smiled and leaned his forehead against hers, taking a moment to let her acceptance sink in. He pulled away slightly as a thought crossed his mind. 'So being with another man who has a son doesn't freak you out any more? Because you know if you take me on, that means you take us both on.'

'Of course,' Hailey said, hurt that he felt he even had to mention it. 'I love Tom, Callum.'

'Even knowing he's not out of the woods yet? Knowing that he could relapse at any time? Knowing that if he does, his diagnosis is not good?'

Hailey swallowed, terrified at the very thought that something could happen to Tom. 'Yes. Even knowing all that. I can't live my life shut away from maybes. Cut myself off from something wonderful because of something that could maybe one day happen. '

'My sentiments exactly.'

'I'm always going to be a little on edge about it, though, Callum. That's just me. But I know he's a little boy who just wants to live his life. I'll try and not be obsessive about it but you're going to have to help me.'

He nuzzled her hair. 'Well, that'll be two of us on edge, then,' he murmured. 'But it'll be my pleasure, helping you to keep everything in perspective.' He found the thought that she would lean on him infinitely comforting. 'Maybe we can be each other's brakes?'

She lifted her face to him and smiled. 'Sounds like a deal.'

'But you have to know,' he said, his fingers stroking her cheeks, 'if it happens it's not anything you've done. It's just life, it's unfair and no one is to blame and we'll deal with it. Together.'

Together. She liked the sound of that. 'Oh, Callum, where have you been all my life? I love you so much.'

He dropped a kiss on her mouth, groaning as her lips opened on his, asking for more. 'Can we stop talking now?' he asked against her mouth.

'I thought you'd never ask,' she whispered, pressing herself against him and letting his kisses sweep her away to a happily ever after.

EPILOGUE

Tom, DRESSED IN HIS little black tuxedo with matching bow-tie, squirmed between Callum and Hailey. 'Can I hold him, please?'

Hailey looked at her sister and Rilla nodded indulgently. She was tired from a lengthy labour but with Luca's arm around her and her son sleeping soundly, she felt strangely invigorated. She'd been so disappointed to miss Hailey's big day but little Carlos had decided he couldn't wait any longer, insisting on arriving on the day of his aunt's wedding.

Hailey, still dressed in her simple white satin slip of a wedding gown, a daisy chain in her hair, moved over and fussed around, getting Tom securely seated between them before handing over her brand-new nephew. They'd come straight from the ceremony when Luca had rung through with the good news.

'What do you reckon, mate?' Callum asked, keeping an arm firmly beneath Tom's for added support.

'Well, he's not as good as a baby brother but I've never had a cousin before so I guess he's all right.'

Rilla laughed. 'Why, thank you young man.'

Callum grinned at Hailey over Tom's head and leaned

across to kiss his wife of two hours. 'Wait till we tell him our news,' he whispered.

Hailey smiled back at her very handsome husband, resplendent in a black tuxedo, looking just as good as the night they'd met. It had been an unorthodox wedding day that had turned into a wonderful double celebration.

Her hand cradled her belly, content in the knowledge that Callum's baby was growing safe and snug. Another Winters baby was going to be making its way in the world in less than eight months. Hopefully, a little brother for Tom.

Life was utterly perfect.

MILLS & BOON®
Pure reading pleasure™

NOVEMBER 2008 HARDBACK TITLES

ROMANCE

The Billionaire's Bride of Vengeance	978 0 263 20382 0
Miranda Lee	
The Santangeli Marriage *Sara Craven*	978 0 263 20383 7
The Spaniard's Virgin Housekeeper	978 0 263 20384 4
Diana Hamilton	
The Greek Tycoon's Reluctant Bride *Kate Hewitt*	978 0 263 20385 1
Innocent Mistress, Royal Wife *Robyn Donald*	978 0 263 20386 8
Taken for Revenge, Bedded for Pleasure	978 0 263 20387 5
India Grey	
The Billionaire Boss's Innocent Bride	978 0 263 20388 2
Lindsay Armstrong	
The Billionaire's Defiant Wife *Amanda Browning*	978 0 263 20389 9
Nanny to the Billionaire's Son *Barbara McMahon*	978 0 263 20390 5
Cinderella and the Sheikh *Natasha Oakley*	978 0 263 20391 2
Promoted: Secretary to Bride! *Jennie Adams*	978 0 263 20392 9
The Black Sheep's Proposal *Patricia Thayer*	978 0 263 20393 6
The Snow-Kissed Bride *Linda Goodnight*	978 0 263 20394 3
The Rancher's Runaway Princess *Donna Alward*	978 0 263 20395 0
The Greek Doctor's New-Year Baby *Kate Hardy*	978 0 263 20396 7
The Wife He's Been Waiting For *Dianne Drake*	978 0 263 20397 4

HISTORICAL

The Captain's Forbidden Miss *Margaret McPhee*	978 0 263 20216 8
The Earl and the Hoyden *Mary Nichols*	978 0 263 20217 5
From Governess to Society Bride *Helen Dickson*	978 0 263 20218 2

MEDICAL™

The Heart Surgeon's Secret Child *Meredith Webber*	978 0 263 19918 5
The Midwife's Little Miracle *Fiona McArthur*	978 0 263 19919 2
The Single Dad's New-Year Bride *Amy Andrews*	978 0 263 19920 8
Posh Doc Claims His Bride *Anne Fraser*	978 0 263 19921 5

⦿™ MILLS & BOON®
Pure reading pleasure™

NOVEMBER 2008 LARGE PRINT TITLES

ROMANCE

Bought for Revenge, Bedded for Pleasure *Emma Darcy*	978 0 263 20090 4
Forbidden: The Billionaire's Virgin Princess *Lucy Monroe*	978 0 263 20091 1
The Greek Tycoon's Convenient Wife *Sharon Kendrick*	978 0 263 20092 8
The Marciano Love-Child *Melanie Milburne*	978 0 263 20093 5
Parents in Training *Barbara McMahon*	978 0 263 20094 2
Newlyweds of Convenience *Jessica Hart*	978 0 263 20095 9
The Desert Prince's Proposal *Nicola Marsh*	978 0 263 20096 6
Adopted: Outback Baby *Barbara Hannay*	978 0 263 20097 3

HISTORICAL

The Virtuous Courtesan *Mary Brendan*	978 0 263 20172 7
The Homeless Heiress *Anne Herries*	978 0 263 20173 4
Rebel Lady, Convenient Wife *June Francis*	978 0 263 20174 1

MEDICAL™

Nurse Bride, Bayside Wedding *Gill Sanderson*	978 0 263 19986 4
Billionaire Doctor, Ordinary Nurse *Carol Marinelli*	978 0 263 19987 1
The Sheikh Surgeon's Baby *Meredith Webber*	978 0 263 19988 8
The Outback Doctor's Surprise Bride *Amy Andrews*	978 0 263 19989 5
A Wedding at Limestone Coast *Lucy Clark*	978 0 263 19990 1
The Doctor's Meant-To-Be Marriage *Janice Lynn*	978 0 263 19991 8

MILLS & BOON®
Pure reading pleasure™

DECEMBER 2008 HARDBACK TITLES

ROMANCE

The Ruthless Magnate's Virgin Mistress *Lynne Graham*	978 0 263 20398 1
The Greek's Forced Bride *Michelle Reid*	978 0 263 20399 8
The Sheikh's Rebellious Mistress *Sandra Marton*	978 0 263 20400 1
The Prince's Waitress Wife *Sarah Morgan*	978 0 263 20401 8
Bought for the Sicilian Billionaire's Bed *Sharon Kendrick*	978 0 263 20402 5
Count Maxime's Virgin *Susan Stephens*	978 0 263 20403 2
The Italian's Ruthless Baby Bargain *Margaret Mayo*	978 0 263 20404 9
Valenti's One-Month Mistress *Sabrina Philips*	978 0 263 20405 6
The Australian's Society Bride *Margaret Way*	978 0 263 20406 3
The Royal Marriage Arrangement *Rebecca Winters*	978 0 263 20407 0
Two Little Miracles *Caroline Anderson*	978 0 263 20408 7
Manhattan Boss, Diamond Proposal *Trish Wylie*	978 0 263 20409 4
Her Valentine Blind Date *Raye Morgan*	978 0 263 20410 0
The Bridesmaid and the Billionaire *Shirley Jump*	978 0 263 20411 7
Children's Doctor, Society Bride *Joanna Neil*	978 0 263 20412 4
Outback Doctor, English Bride *Leah Martyn*	978 0 263 20413 1

HISTORICAL

Marrying the Mistress *Juliet Landon*	978 0 263 20219 9
To Deceive a Duke *Amanda McCabe*	978 0 263 20220 5
Knight of Grace *Sophia James*	978 0 263 20221 2

MEDICAL™

The Heart Surgeon's Baby Surprise *Meredith Webber*	978 0 263 19922 2
A Wife for the Baby Doctor *Josie Metcalfe*	978 0 263 19923 9
The Royal Doctor's Bride *Jessica Matthews*	978 0 263 19924 6
Surgeon Boss, Surprise Dad *Janice Lynn*	978 0 263 19925 3

MILLS & BOON®
Pure reading pleasure™

DECEMBER 2008 LARGE PRINT TITLES

ROMANCE

Hired: The Sheikh's Secretary Mistress *Lucy Monroe*	978 0 263 20098 0
The Billionaire's Blackmailed Bride *Jacqueline Baird*	978 0 263 20099 7
The Sicilian's Innocent Mistress *Carole Mortimer*	978 0 263 20100 0
The Sheikh's Defiant Bride *Sandra Marton*	978 0 263 20101 7
Wanted: Royal Wife and Mother *Marion Lennox*	978 0 263 20102 4
The Boss's Unconventional Assistant *Jennie Adams*	978 0 263 20103 1
Inherited: Instant Family *Judy Christenberry*	978 0 263 20104 8
The Prince's Secret Bride *Raye Morgan*	978 0 263 20105 5

HISTORICAL

Miss Winthorpe's Elopement *Christine Merrill*	978 0 263 20175 8
The Rake's Unconventional Mistress *Juliet Landon*	978 0 263 20176 5
Rags-to-Riches Bride *Mary Nichols*	978 0 263 20177 2

MEDICAL™

Single Dad Seeks a Wife *Melanie Milburne*	978 0 263 19992 5
Her Four-Year Baby Secret *Alison Roberts*	978 0 263 19993 2
Country Doctor, Spring Bride *Abigail Gordon*	978 0 263 19994 9
Marrying the Runaway Bride *Jennifer Taylor*	978 0 263 19995 6
The Midwife's Baby *Fiona McArthur*	978 0 263 19996 3
The Fatherhood Miracle *Margaret Barker*	978 0 263 19997 0